D1046308

The Wrong Grave

Christmas 2009.

KELLY LINK
was born in Florida in
1969 and now lives in
Massachusetts. She has
written two previous
collections of short
stories and has won
three Nebulas and a
World Fantasy Award.
Kelly Link and her
husband Gavin Grant
run a small publishing
company called Small
Beer Press. Her website
is www.kellylink.net

SHAUN TAN
grew up in the northern
suburbs of Perth. He has
written and illustrated
several award-winning
books including *The
Arrival* and *Tales from
Outer Suburbia*. Shaun
Tan lives in Melbourne
with his partner Inari
Kiuru and a small
parrot. His website is
www.shauntan.net

THE
WRONG GRAVE

KELLY LINK

WITH DECORATIONS BY
SHAUN TAN

TEXT PUBLISHING MELBOURNE AUSTRALIA

The paper in this book is manufactured only from wood
grown in sustainable regrowth forests.

The Text Publishing Company
Swann House
22 William Street
Melbourne Victoria 3000
Australia
www.textpublishing.com.au

Copyright © Kelly Link 2008
www.kellylink.net
Illustrations copyright © Shaun Tan 2008

All rights reserved. Without limiting the rights under copyright above, no part of
this publication shall be reproduced, stored in or introduced into a retrieval system,
or transmitted in any form or by any means (electronic, mechanical, photocopying,
recording or otherwise), without the prior permission of both the copyright owner
and the publisher of this book.

First published by Viking, a member of the Penguin Group (USA) Inc. 2008
This edition published by The Text Publishing Company 2009

'The Wrong Grave' first appeared in *The Restless Dead: Ten Original Stories of the
Supernatural*, edited by Deborah Noyes, published by Candlewick Press, 2007.

'The Wizards of Perfil' first appeared in *Firebirds Rising: An Anthology of Original Science
Fiction and Fantasy*, edited by Sharyn November, published by Firebird, an imprint of
Penguin Group (USA) Inc., 2006.

'Magic for Beginners' first appeared in *Magic for Beginners*, published by Small Beer
Press, 2005.

'The Faery Handbag' first appeared in *The Faery Reel: Tales from the Twilight Realm*,
edited by Ellen Datlow and Terri Windling, published by Viking, a division of
Penguin Young Readers Group, 2004.

'The Specialist's Hat' first appeared in *Event Horizon* in 1998; reprinted by permission
of Small Beer Press, 2001.

Cover & preliminaries designed by WH Chong
Page design by Jim Hoover
Printed and bound in Australia by Griffin Press

National Library of Australia
Cataloguing-in-Publication data:

Link, Kelly.

The wrong grave / Kelly Link.

ISBN: 9781921520730 (pbk.)

For secondary school age.

813.6

for Annabel Jones Link

CONTENTS

Anyone might accidentally dig up the wrong grave.

THE WRONG GRAVE

ALL OF THIS happened because a boy I once knew named Miles Sperry decided to go into the resurrectionist business and dig up the grave of his girlfriend, Bethany Baldwin, who had been dead for not quite a year. Miles planned to do this in order to recover the sheaf of poems he had, in what he'd felt was a beautiful and romantic gesture, put into her casket. Or possibly it had just been a really dumb thing to do. He hadn't made copies. Miles had always been impulsive. I think you should know that right up front.

He'd tucked the poems, handwritten, tear-stained and with cross-outs, under Bethany's hands. Her fingers had felt like candles, fat and waxy and pleasantly cool, until you remembered that they were fingers. And he couldn't help noticing that there was something wrong about her breasts, they seemed larger. If Bethany had known that she was going to die, would she have gone all the way with him? One of his poems was about that, about how now they never would, how it was too late now. Carpe diem before you run out of diem.

Bethany's eyes were closed, someone had done that, too, just like they'd arranged her hands, and even her smile looked composed, in the wrong sense of the word. Miles wasn't sure how you made someone smile after they were dead. Bethany didn't look much like she had when she'd been alive. That had been only a few days ago. Now she seemed smaller, and also, oddly, larger. It was the nearest Miles had ever been to a dead person, and he stood there, looking at Bethany, wishing two things: that he was dead, too, and also that it had seemed appropriate to bring along his notebook and a pen. He felt he should be taking notes. After all, this was the most significant thing that had ever happened to Miles. A great change was occurring within him, moment by singular moment.

Poets were supposed to be in the moment, and also stand outside the moment, looking in. For example, Miles had never noticed before, but Bethany's ears were slightly lopsided. One was smaller and slightly higher up. Not that he would have cared, or written a poem about it, or even mentioned it to her, ever, in case it made her self-conscious, but it was a fact and now that he'd noticed it he thought it might have driven him crazy, not mentioning it: he bent over and kissed Bethany's forehead, breathing in. She smelled like a new car. Miles's mind was full of poetic thoughts. Every cloud had a silver lining, except there was probably a more interesting and meaningful way to say that, and death wasn't really a cloud. He thought about what it was: more like an earthquake, maybe, or falling from a great height and smacking into the ground, really hard, which knocked the wind out of you and made it hard to sleep or wake up or eat or care about things like homework or whether there was anything good on TV. And death was foggy, too, but also prickly, so maybe instead of a cloud, a fog made of little sharp things. Needles. Every death fog has a lot of silver needles. Did that make sense? Did it scan?

Then the thought came to Miles like the tolling of a large and leaden bell that Bethany was dead. This may sound strange, but in my experience it's strange and it's also just how it works. You wake up and you remember that the person you loved is dead. And then you think: really?

Then you think how strange it is, how you have to remind yourself that the person you loved is dead, and even while you're thinking about that, the thought comes to you again that the person you loved is dead. And it's the same stupid fog, the same needles or mallet to the intestines or whatever worse thing you want to call it, all over again. But you'll see for yourself someday.

Miles stood there, remembering, until Bethany's mother, Mrs. Baldwin, came up beside him. Her eyes were dry, but her hair was a mess. She'd only managed to put eye shadow on one eyelid. She was wearing jeans and one of Bethany's old T-shirts. Not even one of Bethany's favorite T-shirts. Miles felt embarrassed for her, and for Bethany, too.

"What's that?" Mrs. Baldwin said. Her voice sounded rusty and outlandish, as if she were translating from some other language. Something Indo-Germanic, perhaps.

"My poems. Poems I wrote for her," Miles said. He felt very solemn. This was a historic moment. One day Miles's biographers would write about this. "Three haikus, a sestina, and two villanelles. Some longer pieces. No one else will ever read them."

Mrs. Baldwin looked into Miles's face with her terrible, dry eyes. "I see," she said. "She said you were a lousy poet." She put her hand down into the casket, smoothed Bethany's favorite dress, the one with spider webs, and several holes through which you could see Bethany's itchy black tights. She patted Bethany's hands, and said, "Well, good-bye, old girl. Don't forget to send a postcard."

Don't ask me what she meant by this. Sometimes Bethany's mother said strange things. She was a lapsed Buddhist and a substitute math teacher. Once she'd caught Miles cheating on an algebra quiz. Relations between Miles and Mrs. Baldwin had not improved during the time that Bethany and Miles were dating, and Miles couldn't decide whether or not to believe her about Bethany not liking his poetry. Substitute teachers had strange senses of humor when they had them at all.

He almost reached into the casket and took his poetry back. But Mrs. Baldwin would have thought that she'd proved something; that she'd won. Not that this was a situation where anyone was going to win anything. This was a funeral, not a game show. Nobody was going to get to take Bethany home.

Mrs. Baldwin looked at Miles and Miles looked back. Bethany wasn't looking at anyone. The two people that Bethany had loved most in the world could see, through that dull hateful fog, what the other was thinking, just for a minute, and although you weren't there and even if you had been you wouldn't have known what they were thinking anyway, I'll tell you. I wish it had been me, Miles thought. And Mrs. Baldwin thought, I wish it had been you, too.

Miles put his hands into the pockets of his new suit, turned, and left Mrs. Baldwin standing there. He went and sat next to his own mother, who was trying very hard not to cry. She'd liked Bethany. Everyone had liked Bethany. A few rows in front, a girl named April Lamb was picking her nose in some kind of frenzy of grief. When they got to the cemetery, there was another funeral service going on, the burial of the girl who had been in the other car, and the two groups of mourners glared at each other as they parked their cars and tried to figure out which grave site to gather around.

Two florists had misspelled Bethany's name on the ugly wreaths, BERTHANY and also BETHONY, just like tribe members did when they were voting each other out on the television show *Survivor*, which had always been Bethany's favorite thing about *Survivor*. Bethany had been an excellent speller, although the Lutheran minister who was conducting the sermon didn't mention that.

Miles had an uncomfortable feeling: he became aware that he couldn't wait to get home and call Bethany, to tell her all about this, about everything that had happened since she'd died. He sat and waited until the feeling wore off. It was a feeling he was getting used to.

Bethany had liked Miles because he made her laugh. He makes me laugh, too. Miles figured that digging up Bethany's grave, even that would have made her laugh. Bethany had had a great laugh, which went up and up like a clarinetist on an escalator. It wasn't annoying. It had been delightful, if you liked that kind of laugh. It would have made Bethany laugh that Miles Googled grave digging in order to educate himself. He read an Edgar Allan Poe story, he watched several relevant episodes of *Buffy the Vampire Slayer*, and he bought Vicks VapoRub, which you were supposed to apply under your nose. He bought equipment at Target: a special, battery-operated, telescoping shovel, a set of wire cutters, a flashlight, extra batteries for the shovel and flashlight, and even a Velcro headband with a headlamp that came with a special red lens filter, so that you were less likely to be noticed.

Miles printed out a map of the cemetery so that he could find his way to Bethany's grave off Weeping Fish Lane, even—as an acquaintance of mine once remarked—"in the dead of night when naught can be seen, so pitch is the dark." (Not that the dark would be very pitch. Miles had picked a night when the moon would be full.) The map was also just in case, because he'd seen movies where the dead rose from their graves. You wanted to have all the exits marked in a situation like that.

He told his mother that he was spending the night at his friend John's house. He told his friend John not to tell his mother anything.

If Miles had Googled "poetry" as well as "digging up graves," he would have discovered that his situation was not without precedent. The poet and painter Dante Gabriel Rossetti also buried his poetry with his dead lover. Rossetti, too, had regretted this gesture, had eventually decided to dig up his lover to get back his poems. I'm telling you this so that you never make the same mistake.

I can't tell you whether Dante Gabriel Rossetti was a better poet than Miles, although Rossetti had a sister, Christina Rossetti, who was really something. But you're not interested in my views on poetry. I know you better than that, even if you don't know me. You're waiting for me to get to the part about grave digging.

Miles had a couple of friends and he thought about asking someone to come along on the expedition. But no one except for Bethany knew that Miles wrote poetry. And Bethany had been dead for a while. Eleven months, in fact, which was one month longer than Bethany had been Miles's girlfriend. Long enough that Miles was beginning to make his way out of the fog and the needles. Long enough that he could listen to certain songs on the radio again. Long enough that sometimes there was something dreamlike about his memories of Bethany, as if she'd been a movie that he'd seen a long time ago, late at night on television. Long enough that when he tried to reconstruct the poems he'd written her, especially the villanelle, which had been, in his opinion, really quite good, he couldn't. It was as if when he'd put those poems into the casket, he hadn't just given Bethany the only copies of some poems, but had instead given away those shining, perfect lines, given them away so thoroughly that he'd never be able to write them out again. Miles knew that Bethany was dead. There was nothing to do about that. But the poetry was different. You have to salvage what you can, even if you're the one who buried it in the first place.

You might think at certain points in this story that I'm being hard on Miles, that I'm not sympathetic to his situation. This isn't true. I'm as fond of Miles as I am of anyone else. I don't think he's any stupider or any bit less special or remarkable than—for example—you. Anyone might accidentally dig up the wrong grave. It's a mistake anyone could make.

The moon was full and the map was easy to read even without the aid of the flashlight. The cemetery was full of cats. Don't ask me why. Miles was not afraid. He was resolute. The battery-operated telescoping shovel at first refused to untelescope. He'd tested it in his own backyard, but here, in the cemetery, it seemed unbearably loud. It scared off the cats for a while, but it didn't draw any unwelcome attention. The cats came back. Miles set aside the moldering wreaths and bouquets, and then he used his wire cutters to trace a rectangle. He stuck the telescoping shovel under and pried up fat squares of sod above Bethany's grave. He stacked them up like carpet samples and got to work.

By two A.M., Miles had knotted a length of rope at short, regular intervals for footholds, and then looped it around a tree, so he'd be able to climb out of the grave again, once he'd retrieved his poetry. He was waist-deep in the hole he'd made. The night was warm and he was sweating. It was hard work, directing the shovel. Every once in a while it telescoped while he was using it. He'd borrowed his mother's gardening gloves to keep from getting blisters, but still his hands were getting tired. The gloves were too big. His arms ached.

By three thirty, Miles could no longer see out of the grave in any direction except up. A large white cat came and peered down at Miles, grew bored and left again. The moon moved over Miles's head like a spotlight. He began to wield the shovel more carefully. He didn't want to damage Bethany's casket. When the shovel struck something that was not dirt, Miles remembered that he'd left the Vicks VapoRub on his bed at home. He improvised with a cherry ChapStick he found in his pocket. Now he used his garden-gloved hands to dig and to smooth dirt away. The bloody light emanating from his Velcro headband picked out the ingenious telescoping ridges of the discarded shovel, the little rocks and worms and worm-like roots that poked out of the dirt walls of Miles's excavation, the smoother lid of Bethany's casket.

Miles realized he was standing on the lid. Perhaps he should have made the hole a bit wider. It would be difficult to get the lid open while standing on it. He needed to pee: there was that as well. When he came back, he shone his flashlight into the grave. It seemed to him that the lid of the coffin was slightly ajar. Was that possible? Had he damaged the hinges with the telescoping shovel, or kicked the lid askew somehow when he was shimmying up the rope? He essayed a slow, judicious sniff, but all he smelled was dirt and cherry ChapStick. He applied more cherry ChapStick. Then he lowered himself down into the grave.

The lid wobbled when he tested it with his feet. He decided that if he kept hold of the rope, and slid his foot down and under the lid, like so, then perhaps he could cantilever the lid up—

It was very strange. It felt as if something had hold of his foot. He tried to tug it free, but no, his foot was stuck, caught in some kind of vise or grip. He lowered the toe of his other hiking boot down into the black gap between the coffin and its lid, and tentatively poked it forward, but this produced no result. He'd have to let go of the rope and lift the lid with his hands. Balance like so, carefully, carefully, on the thin rim of the casket. Figure out how he was caught.

It was hard work, balancing and lifting at the same time, although the one foot was still firmly wedged in its accidental toehold. Miles became aware of his own breathing, the furtive scuffling noise of his other boot against the coffin lid. Even the red beam of his lamp as it pitched and swung, back and forth, up and down in the narrow space, seemed unutterably noisy. "Shit, shit, shit," Miles whispered. It was either that or else scream. He got his fingers under the lid of the coffin on either side of his feet and bent his wobbly knees so he wouldn't hurt his back, lifting. Something touched the fingers of his right hand.

No, his fingers had touched something. *Don't be ridiculous, Miles.* He yanked the lid up as fast and hard as he could, the way

9

you would rip off a bandage if you suspected there were baby spiders hatching under it. "Shit, shit, shit, shit, shit!"

He yanked and someone else pushed. The lid shot up and fell back against the opposite embankment of dirt. The dead girl who had hold of Miles's boot let go.

This was the first of the many unexpected and unpleasant shocks that Miles was to endure for the sake of poetry. The second was the sickening—no, shocking—shock that he had dug up the wrong grave, the wrong dead girl.

The wrong dead girl was lying there, smiling up at him, and her eyes were open. She was several years older than Bethany. She was taller and had a significantly more developed rack. She even had a tattoo.

The smile of the wrong dead girl was white and orthodontically perfected. Bethany had had braces that turned kissing into a heroic feat. You had to kiss around braces, slide your tongue up or sideways or under, like navigating through barbed wire: a delicious, tricky trip through No Man's Land. Bethany pursed her mouth forward when she kissed. If Miles forgot and mashed his lips down too hard on hers, she whacked him on the back of his head. This was one of the things about his relationship with Bethany that Miles remembered vividly, looking down at the wrong dead girl.

The wrong dead girl spoke first. "Knock knock," she said.

"What?" Miles said.

"Knock knock," the wrong dead girl said again.

"Who's there?" Miles said.

"Gloria," the wrong dead girl said. "Gloria Palnick. Who are you and what are you doing in my grave?"

"This isn't your grave," Miles said, aware that he was arguing with a dead girl, and the wrong dead girl at that. "This is

Bethany's grave. What are you doing in Bethany's grave?"

"Oh no," Gloria Palnick said. "This is my grave and I get to ask the questions."

A notion crept, like little dead cat feet, over Miles. Possibly he had made a dangerous and deeply embarrassing mistake. "Poetry," he managed to say. "There was some poetry that I, ah, that I accidentally left in my girlfriend's casket. And there's a deadline for a poetry contest coming up, and so I really, really needed to get it back."

The dead girl stared at him. There was something about her hair that Miles didn't like.

"Excuse me, but are you for real?" she said. "This sounds like one of those lame excuses. The dog ate my homework. I accidentally buried my poetry with my dead girlfriend."

"Look," Miles said, "I checked the tombstone and everything. This is supposed to be Bethany's grave. Bethany Baldwin. I'm really sorry I bothered you and everything, but this isn't really my fault." The dead girl just stared at him thoughtfully. He wished that she would blink. She wasn't smiling anymore. Her hair, lank and black, where Bethany's had been brownish and frizzy in summer, was writhing a little, like snakes. Miles thought of centipedes. Inky midnight tentacles.

"Maybe I should just go away," Miles said. "Leave you to, ah, rest in peace or whatever."

"I don't think sorry cuts the mustard here," Gloria Palnick said. She barely moved her mouth when she spoke, Miles noticed. And yet her enunciation was fine. "Besides, I'm sick of this place. It's boring. Maybe I'll just come along with."

"What?" Miles said. He felt behind himself, surreptitiously, for the knotted rope.

"I said, maybe I'll come with you," Gloria Palnick said. She sat up. Her hair was really coiling around, really seething now. Miles thought he could hear hissing noises.

"You can't do that!" he said. "I'm sorry, but no. Just no."

"Well then, you stay here and keep me company," Gloria Palnick said. Her hair was really something.

"I can't do that either," Miles said, trying to explain quickly, before the dead girl's hair decided to strangle him. "I'm going to be a poet. It would be a great loss to the world if I never got a chance to publish my poetry."

"I see," Gloria Palnick said, as if she did, in fact, see a great deal. Her hair settled back down on her shoulders and began to act a lot more like hair. "You don't want me to come home with you. You don't want to stay here with me. Then how about this? If you're such a great poet, then write me a poem. Write something about me so that everyone will be sad that I died."

"I could do that," Miles said. Relief bubbled up through his middle like tiny doughnuts in an industrial deep-fat fryer. "Let's do that. You lie down and make yourself comfortable and I'll rebury you. Today I've got a quiz in American History, and I was going to study for it during my free period after lunch, but I could write a poem for you instead."

"Today is Saturday," the dead girl said.

"Oh, hey," Miles said. "Then no problem. I'll go straight home and work on your poem. Should be done by Monday."

"Not so fast," Gloria Palnick said. "You need to know all about my life and about me, if you're going to write a poem about me, right? And how do I know you'll write a poem if I let you bury me again? How will I know if the poem's any good? No dice. I'm coming home with you and I'm sticking around until I get my poem. 'Kay?"

She stood up. She was several inches taller than Miles. "Do

you have any ChapStick?" she said. "My lips are really dry."

"Here," Miles said. Then, "You can keep it."

"Oh, afraid of dead girl cooties," Gloria Palnick said. She smacked her lips at him in an upsetting way.

"I'll climb up first," Miles said. He had the idea that if he could just get up the rope, if he could yank the rope up after himself fast enough, he might be able to run away, get to the fence where he'd chained up his bike, before Gloria managed to get out. It wasn't like she knew where he lived. She didn't even know his name.

"Fine," Gloria said. She looked like she knew what Miles was thinking and didn't really care. By the time Miles had bolted up the rope, yanking it up out of the grave, abandoning the telescoping shovel, the wire cutters, the wronged dead girl, and had unlocked his road bike and was racing down the empty 5 A.M. road, the little red dot of light from his headlamp falling into potholes, he'd almost managed to persuade himself that it had all been a grisly hallucination. Except for the fact that the dead girl's cold dead arms were around his waist, suddenly, and her cold dead face was pressed against his back, her damp hair coiling around his head and tapping at his mouth, burrowing down his filthy shirt.

"Don't leave me like that again," she said.

"No," Miles said. "I won't. Sorry."

He couldn't take the dead girl home. He couldn't think of how to explain it to his parents. No, no, no. He didn't want to take her over to John's house either. It was far too complicated. Not just the girl, but he was covered in dirt. John wouldn't be able to keep his big mouth shut.

"Where are we going?" the dead girl said.

"I know a place," Miles said. "Could you please not put your hands under my shirt? They're really cold. And your fingernails are kind of sharp."

"Sorry," the dead girl said.

They rode along in silence until they were passing the 7-Eleven at the corner of Eighth and Walnut, and the dead girl said, "Could we stop for a minute? I'd like some beef jerky. And a Diet Coke."

Miles braked. "Beef jerky?" he said. "Is that what dead people eat?"

"It's the preservatives," the dead girl said, somewhat obscurely.

Miles gave up. He steered the bike into the parking lot. "Let go, please," he said. The dead girl let go. He got off the bike and turned around. He'd been wondering just exactly how she'd managed to sit behind him on the bike, and he saw that she was sitting above the rear tire on a cushion of her horrible, shiny hair. Her legs were stretched out on either side, toes in black combat boots floating just above the asphalt, and yet the bike didn't fall over. It just hung there under her. For the first time in almost a month, Miles found himself thinking about Bethany as if she were still alive: Bethany is never going to believe this. But then, Bethany had never believed in anything like ghosts. She'd hardly believed in the school dress code. She definitely wouldn't have believed in a dead girl who could float around on her hair like it was an anti-gravity device.

"I can also speak fluent Spanish," Gloria Palnick said.

Miles reached into his back pocket for his wallet, and discovered that the pocket was full of dirt. "I can't go in there," he said. "For one thing, I'm a kid and it's five in the morning. Also I look like I just escaped from a gang of naked mole rats. I'm filthy."

The dead girl just looked at him. He said, coaxingly, "*You* should go in. You're older. I'll give you all the money I've got. You go in and I'll stay out here and work on the poem."

"You'll ride off and leave me here," the dead girl said. She didn't sound angry, just matter of fact. But her hair was beginning to float up. It lifted her up off Miles's bike in a kind of hairy cloud and then plaited itself down her back in a long, business-like rope.

"I won't," Miles promised. "Here. Take this. Buy whatever you want."

Gloria Palnick took the money. "How very generous of you," she said.

"No problem," Miles told her. "I'll wait here." And he did wait. He waited until Gloria Palnick went into the 7-Eleven. Then he counted to thirty, waited one second more, got back on his bike and rode away. By the time he'd made it to the meditation cabin in the woods back behind Bethany's mother's house, where he and Bethany had liked to sit and play Monopoly, Miles felt as if things were under control again, more or less. There is nothing so calming as a meditation cabin where long, boring games of Monopoly have taken place. He'd clean up in the cabin sink, and maybe take a nap. Bethany's mother never went out there. Her ex-husband's meditation clothes, his scratchy prayer mat, all his Buddhas and scrolls and incense holders and posters of Che Guevara were still out here. Miles had snuck into the cabin a few times since Bethany's death, to sit in the dark and listen to the plink-plink of the meditation fountain and think about things. He was sure Bethany's mother wouldn't have minded if she knew, although he hadn't ever asked, just in case. Which had been wise of him.

The key to the cabin was on the beam just above the door, but he didn't need it after all. The door stood open. There was a smell of incense, and of other things: cherry ChapStick and dirt and beef jerky. There was a pair of black combat boots beside the door.

Miles squared his shoulders. I have to admit that he was behaving sensibly here, finally. Finally. Because—and Miles and I are in agreement for once—if the dead girl could follow him somewhere before he even knew exactly where he was going, then there was no point in running away. Anywhere he went she'd already be there. Miles took off his shoes, because you were supposed to take off your shoes when you went into the cabin. It was a gesture of respect. He put them down beside the combat boots and went inside. The waxed pine floor felt silky under his bare feet. He looked down and saw that he was walking on Gloria Palnick's hair.

"Sorry!" Miles said. He meant several things by that. He meant sorry for walking on your hair. Sorry for riding off and leaving you in the 7-Eleven after promising that I wouldn't. Sorry for the grave wrong I've done you. But most of all he meant sorry, dead girl, that I ever dug you up in the first place.

"Don't mention it," the dead girl said. "Want some jerky?"

"Sure," he said. He felt he had no other choice.

He was beginning to feel he would have liked this dead girl under other circumstances, despite her annoying, bullying hair. She had poise. A sense of humor. She seemed to have what his mother called stick-to-itiveness; what the AP English Exam prefers to call tenacity. Miles recognized the quality. He had it in no small degree himself. The dead girl was also extremely pretty, if you ignored the hair. You might think less of Miles that he thought so well of the dead girl, that this was a betrayal of Bethany. *Miles* felt it was a betrayal. But he thought that Bethany might have liked the dead girl too. She would certainly have liked her tattoo.

"How is the poem coming?" the dead girl said.

"There's not a lot that rhymes with Gloria," Miles said. "Or Palnick."

"Toothpick," said the dead girl. There was a fragment of jerky caught in her teeth. "Euphoria."

"Maybe *you* should write the stupid poem," Miles said. There was an awkward pause, broken only by the almost-noiseless glide of hair retreating across a pine floor. Miles sat down, sweeping the floor with his hand, just in case.

"You were going to tell me something about your life," he said.

"Boring," Gloria Palnick said. "Short. Over."

"That's not much to work with. Unless you want a haiku."

"Tell me about this girl you were trying to dig up," Gloria said. "The one you wrote the poetry for."

"Her name was Bethany," Miles said. "She died in a car crash."

"Was she pretty?" Gloria said.

"Yeah," Miles said.

"You liked her a lot," Gloria said.

"Yeah," Miles said.

"Are you sure you're a poet?" Gloria asked.

Miles was silent. He gnawed his jerky ferociously. It tasted like dirt. Maybe he'd write a poem about it. That would show Gloria Palnick.

He swallowed and said, "Why were you in Bethany's grave?"

"How should I know?" she said. She was sitting across from him, leaning against a concrete Buddha the size of a three-year-old, but much fatter and holier. Her hair hung down over her face, just like a Japanese horror movie. "What do you think, that Bethany and I swapped coffins, just for fun?"

"Is Bethany like you?" Miles said. "Does she have weird hair and follow people around and scare them just for fun?"

"No," the dead girl said through her hair. "Not for fun. But what's wrong with having a little fun? It gets dull. And why should we stop having fun, just because we're dead? It's not all demon cocktails and Scrabble down in the old bardo, you know?"

"You know what's weird?" Miles said. "You sound like her. Bethany. You say the same kind of stuff."

"It was dumb to try to get your poems back," said the dead girl. "You can't just give something to somebody and then take it back again."

"I just miss her," Miles said. He began to cry.

After a while, the dead girl got up and came over to him. She took a big handful of her hair and wiped his face with it. It was soft and absorbent and it made Miles's skin crawl. He stopped crying, which might have been what the dead girl was hoping. "Go home," she said.

Miles shook his head. "No," he finally managed to say. He was shivering like crazy.

"Why not?" the dead girl said.

"Because I'll go home and you'll be there, waiting for me."

"I won't," the dead girl said. "I promise."

"Really?" Miles said.

"I really promise," said the dead girl. "I'm sorry I teased you, Miles."

"That's okay," Miles said. He got up and then he just stood there, looking down at her. He seemed to be about to ask her something, and then he changed his mind. She could see this happen, and she could see why, too. He knew he ought to leave now, while she was willing to let him go. He didn't want to fuck up by asking something impossible and obvious and stupid. That was okay by her. She couldn't be sure that he wouldn't say something that would rile up her hair. Not to mention the tattoo. She didn't think he'd noticed when her tattoo had started getting annoyed.

"Good-bye," Miles said at last. It almost looked as if he wanted her to shake his hand, but when she sent out a length of her hair, he turned and ran. It was a little disappointing. And the dead girl couldn't help but notice that he'd left his shoes and his bike behind.

The dead girl walked around the cabin, picking things up and putting them down again. She kicked the Monopoly box, which was a game that she'd always hated. That was one of the okay things about being dead, that nobody ever wanted to play Monopoly.

At last she came to the statue of St. Francis, whose head had been knocked right off during an indoor game of croquet a long time ago. Bethany Baldwin had made St. Francis a lumpy substitute Ganesh head out of modeling clay. You could lift that clay elephant head off, and there was a hollow space where Miles and Bethany had left secret things for each other. The dead girl reached down her shirt and into the cavity where her more interesting and useful organs had once been (she had been an organ donor). She'd put Miles's poetry in there for safekeeping.

She folded up the poetry, wedged it inside St. Francis, and fixed the Ganesh head back on. Maybe Miles would find it someday. She would have liked to see the look on his face.

We don't often get a chance to see our dead. Still less often do we know them when we see them. Mrs. Baldwin's eyes opened. She looked up and saw the dead girl and smiled. She said, "Bethany."

Bethany sat down on her mother's bed. She took her mother's hand. If Mrs. Baldwin thought Bethany's hand was cold, she didn't say so. She held on tightly. "I was dreaming about you," she told Bethany. "You were in an Andrew Lloyd Webber musical."

"It was just a dream," Bethany said.

Mrs. Baldwin reached up and touched a piece of Bethany's hair with her other hand. "You've changed your hair," she said. "I like it."

They were both silent. Bethany's hair stayed very still. Perhaps it felt flattered.

"Thank you for coming back," Mrs. Baldwin said at last.

"I can't stay," Bethany said.

Mrs. Baldwin held her daughter's hand tighter. "I'll go with you. That's why you've come, isn't it? Because I'm dead too?"

Bethany shook her head. "No. Sorry. You're not dead. It's Miles's fault. He dug me up."

"He did what?" Mrs. Baldwin said. She forgot the small, lowering unhappiness of discovering that she was not dead after all.

"He wanted his poetry back," Bethany said. "The poems he gave me."

"That idiot," Mrs. Baldwin said. It was exactly the sort of thing she expected of Miles, but only with the advantage of hindsight, because how could you really expect such a thing. "What did you do to him?"

"I played a good joke on him," Bethany said. She'd never really tried to explain her relationship with Miles to her mother. It seemed especially pointless now. She wriggled her fingers, and her mother instantly let go of Bethany's hand.

Being a former Buddhist, Mrs. Baldwin had always understood that when you hold onto your children too tightly, you end up pushing them away instead. Except that after Bethany had died, she wished she'd held on a little tighter. She drank up Bethany with her eyes. She noted the tattoo on Bethany's arm with both disapproval and delight. Disapproval, because one day Bethany might regret getting a tattoo of a cobra that wrapped all the way around her bicep. Delight, because something about the tattoo suggested Bethany was really here. That this wasn't just a dream. Andrew Lloyd Webber musicals were one thing. But she would never have dreamed that her daughter was alive again and tattooed and wearing long, writhing, midnight tails of hair.

"I have to go," Bethany said. She had turned her head a little, towards the window, as if she were listening for something far away.

"Oh," her mother said, trying to sound as if she didn't mind. She didn't want to ask: Will you come back? She was a lapsed Buddhist, but not so very lapsed, after all. She was still working to relinquish all desire, all hope, all self. When a person like Mrs. Baldwin suddenly finds that her life has been dismantled by a great catastrophe, she may then hold on to her belief as if to a life raft, even if the belief is this: that one should hold on to nothing. Mrs. Baldwin had taken her Buddhism very seriously, once, before substitute teaching had knocked it out of her.

Bethany stood up. "I'm sorry I wrecked the car," she said, although this wasn't completely true. If she'd still been alive, she would have been sorry. But she was dead. She didn't know how to be sorry anymore. And the longer she stayed, the more likely it seemed that her hair would do something truly terrible. Her hair was not good Buddhist hair. It did not love the living world or the things in the living world, and it *did not love them* in an utterly unenlightened way. There was nothing of light or enlightenment about Bethany's hair. It knew nothing of hope, but it had desires and ambitions. It's best not to speak of those ambitions. As for the tattoo, it wanted to be left alone. And to be allowed to eat people, just every once in a while.

When Bethany stood up, Mrs. Baldwin said suddenly, "I've been thinking I might give up substitute teaching."

Bethany waited.

"I might go to Japan to teach English," Mrs. Baldwin said. "Sell the house, just pack up and go. Is that okay with you? Do you mind?"

Bethany didn't mind. She bent over and kissed her mother on her forehead. She left a smear of cherry ChapStick. When she had gone, Mrs. Baldwin got up and put on her bathrobe, the one with white cranes and frogs. She went downstairs and made coffee and sat at the kitchen table for a long time, staring at nothing. Her coffee got cold and she never even noticed.

The dead girl left town as the sun was coming up. I won't tell you where she went. Maybe she joined the circus and took part in daring trapeze acts that put her hair to good use, kept it from getting bored and plotting the destruction of all that is good and pure and lovely. Maybe she shaved her head and went on a pilgrimage to some remote lamasery and came back as a superhero with a dark past and some kick-ass martial-arts moves. Maybe she sent her mother postcards from time to time. Maybe she wrote them as part of her circus act, using the tips of her hair, dipping them into an inkwell. These postcards, not to mention her calligraphic scrolls, are highly sought after by collectors nowadays. I have two.

Miles stopped writing poetry for several years. He never went back to get his bike. He stayed away from graveyards and also from girls with long hair. The last I heard, he had a job writing topical haikus for the Weather Channel. One of his best-known haikus is the one about tropical storm Suzy. It goes something like this:

A young girl passes
in a hurry. Hair uncombed.
Full of black devils.

Wizards are always hungry.

THE WIZARDS OF PERFIL

THE WOMAN WHO sold leech grass baskets and pickled beets in the Perfil market took pity on Onion's aunt. "On your own, my love?"

Onion's aunt nodded. She was still holding out the earrings which she'd hoped someone would buy. There was a train leaving in the morning for Qual, but the tickets were dear. Her daughter Halsa, Onion's cousin, was sulking. She'd wanted the earrings for herself. The twins held hands and stared about the market.

Onion thought the beets were more beautiful than the earrings, which had belonged to his mother. The beets were rich and velvety and mysterious as pickled stars in shining jars. Onion had had nothing to eat all day. His stomach was empty, and his head was full of the thoughts of the people in the market: Halsa thinking of the earrings, the market woman's disinterested kindness, his aunt's dull worry. There was a man at another stall whose wife was sick. She was coughing up blood. A girl went by. She was thinking about a man who had gone to the war. The man wouldn't come back. Onion went back to thinking about the beets.

"Just you to look after all these children," the market woman said. "These are bad times. Where's your lot from?"

"Come from Labbit, and Larch before that," Onion's aunt said. "We're trying to get to Qual. My husband had family there. I have these earrings and these candlesticks."

The woman shook her head. "No one will buy these," she said. "Not for any good price. The market is full of refugees selling off their bits and pieces."

Onion's aunt said, "Then what should I do?" She didn't seem to expect an answer, but the woman said, "There's a man who comes to the market today, who buys children for the wizards of Perfil. He pays good money and they say that the children are treated well."

All wizards are strange, but the wizards of Perfil are strangest of all. They build tall towers in the marshes of Perfil, and there they live like anchorites in lonely little rooms at the top of their towers. They rarely come down at all, and no one is sure what their magic is good for. There are balls of sickly green fire that dash around the marshes at night, hunting for who knows what, and sometimes a tower tumbles down and then the prickly reeds and marsh lilies that look like ghostly white hands grow up over the tumbled stones and the marsh mud sucks the rubble down.

Everyone knows that there are wizard bones under the marsh mud and that the fish and the birds that live in the marsh are strange creatures. They have got magic in them. Children dare each other to go into the marsh and catch fish. Sometimes when a brave child catches a fish in the murky, muddy marsh pools, the fish will call the child by name and beg to be released. And if you don't let that fish go, it will tell you, gasping for air, when and how you will die. And if you cook the fish and eat it, you will dream wizard dreams. But if you let your fish go, it will tell you a secret.

This is what the people of Perfil say about the wizards of Perfil.

Everyone knows that the wizards of Perfil talk to demons and hate sunlight and have long twitching noses like rats. They never bathe.

Everyone knows that the wizards of Perfil are hundreds and hundreds of years old. They sit and dangle their fishing lines out of the windows of their towers and they use magic to bait their hooks. They eat their fish raw and they throw the fish bones out of the window the same way that they empty their chamber pots. The wizards of Perfil have filthy habits and no manners at all.

Everyone knows that the wizards of Perfil eat children when they grow tired of fish.

This is what Halsa told her brothers and Onion while Onion's aunt bargained in the Perfil markets with the wizard's secretary.

The wizard's secretary was a man named Tolcet and he wore a sword in his belt. He was a black man with white-pink spatters on his face and across the backs of his hands. Onion had never seen a man who was two colors.

Tolcet gave Onion and his cousins pieces of candy. He said to Onion's aunt, "Can any of them sing?"

Onion's aunt indicated that the children should sing. The

twins, Mik and Bonti, had strong, clear soprano voices, and when Halsa sang, everyone in the market fell silent and listened. Halsa's voice was like honey and sunlight and sweet water.

Onion loved to sing, but no one loved to hear it. When it was his turn and he opened his mouth to sing, he thought of his mother and tears came to his eyes. The song that came out of his mouth wasn't one he knew. It wasn't even in a proper language and Halsa crossed her eyes and stuck out her tongue. Onion went on singing.

"Enough," Tolcet said. He pointed at Onion. "You sing like a toad, boy. Do you know when to be quiet?"

"He's quiet," Onion's aunt said. "His parents are dead. He doesn't eat much, and he's strong enough. We walked here from Larch. And he's not afraid of witchy folk, begging your pardon. There were no wizards in Larch, but his mother could find things when you lost them. She could charm your cows so that they always came home."

"How old is he?" Tolcet said.

"Eleven," Onion's aunt said, and Tolcet grunted.

"Small for his age." Tolcet looked at Onion. He looked at Halsa, who crossed her arms and scowled hard. "Will you come with me, boy?"

Onion's aunt nudged him. He nodded.

"I'm sorry for it," his aunt said to Onion, "but it can't be helped. I promised your mother I'd see you were taken care of. This is the best I can do."

Onion said nothing. He knew his aunt would have sold Halsa to the wizard's secretary and hoped it was a piece of luck for her daughter. But there was also a part of his aunt that was glad that Tolcet wanted Onion instead. Onion could see it in her mind.

Tolcet paid Onion's aunt twenty-four brass fish, which was

slightly more than it had cost to bury Onion's parents, but slightly less than Onion's father had paid for their best milk cow, two years before. It was important to know how much things were worth. The cow was dead and so was Onion's father.

"Be *good*," Onion's aunt said. "Here. Take this." She gave Onion one of the earrings that had belonged to his mother. It was shaped like a snake. Its writhing tail hooked into its narrow mouth, and Onion had always wondered if the snake was surprised about that, to end up with a mouthful of itself like that, for all eternity. Or maybe it was eternally furious, like Halsa.

Halsa's mouth was screwed up like a button. When she hugged Onion good-bye, she said, "Brat. Give it to me." Halsa had already taken the wooden horse that Onion's father had carved, and Onion's knife, the one with the bone handle.

Onion tried to pull away, but she held him tightly, as if she couldn't bear to let him go. "He wants to eat you," she said. "The wizard will put you in an oven and roast you like a suckling pig. So give me the earring. Suckling pigs don't need earrings."

Onion wriggled away. The wizard's secretary was watching, and Onion wondered if he'd heard Halsa. Of course, anyone who wanted a child to eat would have taken Halsa, not Onion. Halsa was older and bigger and plumper. Then again, anyone who looked hard at Halsa would suspect she would taste sour and unpleasant. The only sweetness in Halsa was in her singing. Even Onion loved to listen to Halsa when she sang.

Mik and Bonti gave Onion shy little kisses on his cheek. He knew they wished the wizard's secretary had bought Halsa instead. Now that Onion was gone, it would be the twins that Halsa pinched and bullied and teased.

Tolcet swung a long leg over his horse. Then he leaned down.

"Come on, boy," he said, and held his speckled hand out to Onion. Onion took it.

The horse was warm and its back was broad and high. There was no saddle and no reins, only a kind of woven harness with a basket on either flank, filled with goods from the market. Tolcet held the horse quiet with his knees, and Onion held on tight to Tolcet's belt.

"That song you sang," Tolcet said. "Where did you learn it?"

"I don't know," Onion said. It came to him that the song had been a song that Tolcet's mother had sung to her son, when Tolcet was a child. Onion wasn't sure what the words meant because Tolcet wasn't sure either. There was something about a lake and a boat, something about a girl who had eaten the moon.

The marketplace was full of people selling things. From his vantage point Onion felt like a prince: as if he could afford to buy anything he saw. He looked down at a stall selling apples and potatoes and hot leek pies. His mouth watered. Over here was an incense seller's stall, and there was a woman telling fortunes. At the train station, people were lining up to buy tickets for Qual. In the morning a train would leave and Onion's aunt and Halsa and the twins would be on it. It was a dangerous passage. There were unfriendly armies between here and Qual. When Onion looked back at his aunt, he knew it would do no good, she would only think he was begging her not to leave him with the wizard's secretary, but he said it all the same: "Don't go to Qual."

But he knew even as he said it that she would go anyway. No one ever listened to Onion.

The horse tossed its head. The wizard's secretary made a *tch-tch* sound and then leaned back in the saddle. He seemed undecided about something. Onion looked back one more time at his aunt. He had never seen her smile once in the two years he'd lived with her, and she did not smile now, even though twenty-four brass fish was not a small sum of money and even though she'd kept her promise to Onion's mother. Onion's mother had smiled often, despite the fact that her teeth were not particularly good.

"He'll eat you," Halsa called to Onion. "Or he'll drown you in the marsh! He'll cut you up into little pieces and bait his fishing line with your fingers!" She stamped her foot.

"Halsa!" her mother said.

"On second thought," Tolcet said, "I'll take the girl. Will you sell her to me instead?"

"What?" Halsa said.

"What?" Onion's aunt said.

"No!" Onion said, but Tolcet drew out his purse again. Halsa, it seemed, was worth more than a small boy with a bad voice. And Onion's aunt needed money badly. So Halsa got up on the horse behind Tolcet, and Onion watched as his bad-tempered cousin rode away with the wizard's servant.

There was a voice in Onion's head. It said, "Don't worry, boy. All will be well and all manner of things will be well." It sounded like Tolcet, a little amused, a little sad.

There is a story about the wizards of Perfil and how one fell in love with a church bell. First he tried to buy it with gold and then, when the church refused his money, he stole it by magic. As the wizard flew back across the marshes, carrying the bell in his arms, he flew too low and the devil reached up and grabbed his heel. The wizard dropped the church bell into the marshes and it sank and was lost forever. Its voice is clappered with mud and moss, and although the wizard never gave up searching for it and calling its name, the bell never answered and the wizard grew thin and died of grief. Fishermen say that the dead wizard still flies over the marsh, crying out for the lost bell.

Everyone knows that wizards are pigheaded and come to bad ends. No wizard has ever made himself useful by magic, or, if they've tried, they've only made matters worse. No wizard has ever stopped a war or mended a fence. It's better that they stay in their marshes, out of the way of worldly folk like farmers and soldiers and merchants and kings.

"Well," Onion's aunt said. She sagged. They could no longer see Tolcet or Halsa. "Come along, then."

They went back through the market and Onion's aunt bought cakes of sweetened rice for the three children. Onion ate his without knowing that he did so: since the wizard's servant had taken away Halsa instead, it felt as if there were two Onions, one Onion here in the market and one Onion riding along with Tolcet and Halsa. He stood and was carried along at the same time and it made him feel terribly dizzy. Market-Onion stumbled, his mouth full of rice, and his aunt caught him by the elbow.

"We don't eat children," Tolcet was saying. "There are plenty of fish and birds in the marshes."

"I know," Halsa said. She sounded sulky. "And the wizards live in houses with lots of stairs. Towers. Because they think they're so much better than anybody else. So above the rest of the world."

"And how do you know about the wizards of Perfil?" Tolcet said.

"The woman in the market," Halsa said. "And the other people in the market. Some are afraid of the wizards and some think that there are no wizards. That they're a story for children. That the marshes are full of runaway slaves and deserters. Nobody knows why wizards would come and build towers in the Perfil marsh, where the ground is like cheese and no one can find them. Why do the wizards live in the marshes?"

"Because the marsh is full of magic," Tolcet said.

"Then why do they build the towers so high?" Halsa said.

"Because wizards are curious," Tolcet said. "They like to be able to see things that are far off. They like to be as close as possible to the stars. And they don't like to be bothered by people who ask lots of questions."

"Why do the wizards buy children?" Halsa said.

"To run up and down the stairs," Tolcet said, "to fetch them water for bathing and to carry messages and to bring them breakfasts and dinners and lunches and suppers. Wizards are always hungry."

"So am I," Halsa said.

"Here," Tolcet said. He gave Halsa an apple. "You see things that are in people's heads. You can see things that are going to happen."

"Yes," Halsa said. "Sometimes." The apple was wrinkled but sweet.

"Your cousin has a gift, too," Tolcet said.

"Onion?" Halsa said scornfully. Onion saw that it had never felt like a gift to Halsa. No wonder she'd hidden it.

"Can you see what is in my head right now?" Tolcet said.

Halsa looked and Onion looked, too. There was no curiosity or fear about in Tolcet's head. There was nothing. There was no Tolcet, no wizard's servant. Only brackish water and lonely white birds flying above it.

It's beautiful, Onion said.

"What?" his aunt said in the market. "Onion? Sit down, child."

"Some people find it so," Tolcet said, answering Onion. Halsa said nothing, but she frowned.

Tolcet and Halsa rode through the town and out of the town gates onto the road that led back toward Labbit and east, where there were more refugees coming and going, day and night. They were mostly women and children and they were afraid. There were rumors of armies behind them. There was a story that, in a fit of madness, the king had killed his youngest son. Onion saw a chess game, a thin-faced, anxious, yellow-haired boy Onion's age moving a black queen across the board, and then the chess pieces scattered across a stone floor. A woman was saying something. The boy bent down to pick up the scattered pieces. The king was laughing. He had a sword in his hand and he brought it down and then there was blood on it. Onion had never seen a king before, although he had seen men with swords. He had seen men with blood on their swords.

Tolcet and Halsa went away from the road, following a wide river, which was less a river than a series of wide, shallow pools. On the other side of the river, muddy paths disappeared into thick stands of rushes and bushes full of berries. There was a feeling of watchfulness, and the cunning, curious stillness of something alive, something half-asleep and half-waiting, a hidden, invisible humming, as if even the air were saturated with magic.

"Berries! Ripe and sweet!" a girl was singing out, over and over again in the market. Onion wished she would be quiet. His aunt bought bread and salt and hard cheese. She piled them into Onion's arms.

"It will be uncomfortable at first," Tolcet was saying. "The marshes of Perfil are so full of magic that they drink up all other kinds of magic. The only ones who work magic in the marshes of Perfil are the wizards of Perfil. And there are bugs."

"I don't want anything to do with magic," Halsa said primly.

Again Onion tried to look in Tolcet's mind, but again all he saw was the marshes. Fat-petaled, waxy, white flowers and crouching trees that dangled their long brown fingers as if fishing. Tolcet laughed. "I can feel you looking," he said. "Don't look too long or you'll fall in and drown."

"I'm not looking!" Halsa said. But she *was* looking. Onion could feel her looking, as if she were turning a key in a door.

The marshes smelled salty and rich, like a bowl of broth. Tolcet's horse ambled along, its hooves sinking into the path. Behind them, water welled up and filled the depressions. Fat jeweled flies clung, vibrating, to the rushes, and once, in a clear pool of water, Onion saw a snake curling like a green ribbon through water weeds soft as a cloud of hair.

"Wait here and watch Bonti and Mik for me," Onion's aunt said. "I'll go to the train station. Onion? Are you all right?"

Onion nodded dreamily.

Tolcet and Halsa rode farther into the marsh, away from the road and the Perfil market and Onion. It was very different from the journey to Perfil, which had been hurried and dusty and dry and on foot. Whenever Onion or one of the twins stumbled or lagged behind, Halsa had rounded them up like a dog chasing sheep, pinching and slapping. It was hard to imagine cruel, greedy, unhappy Halsa being able to pick things out of other people's minds, although she had always seemed to know when Mik or Bonti had found something edible; where there might be a soft piece of ground to sleep; when they should duck off the road because soldiers were coming.

Halsa was thinking of her mother and her brothers. She was thinking about the look on her father's face when the soldiers had shot him behind the barn; the earrings shaped like snakes; how the train to Qual would be blown up by saboteurs. She meant to be on that train, she knew it. She was furious at Tolcet for taking her away; at Onion, because Tolcet had changed his mind about Onion.

Every now and then, while he waited in the market for his aunt to come back, Onion could see the pointy roofs of the wizards' towers leaning against the sky as if they were waiting for him, just beyond the Perfil market, and then the towers would recede, and he would go with them, and find himself again with Tolcet and Halsa. Their path ran up along a canal of tarry water, angled off into thickets of bushes bent down with bright yellow berries, and then returned. It cut across other paths, these narrower and crookeder, overgrown and secret looking. At last they rode through a stand of sweet-smelling trees and came out into a grassy meadow that seemed not much larger than the Perfil market. Up close, the towers were not particularly splendid. They were tumbledown and so close together one might have strung a line for laundry from tower to tower, if wizards had been concerned with such things as laundry. Efforts had been made to buttress the towers; some had long, eccentrically curving fins of strategically piled rocks. There were twelve standing towers that looked as if they might be occupied. Others were half in ruins or were only piles of lichen-encrusted rocks that had already been scavenged for useful building materials.

Around the meadow were more paths: worn, dirt paths and canals that sank into branchy, briary tangles, some so low that a boat would never have passed without catching. Even a swimmer would have to duck her head. Children sat on the ruined walls of toppled towers and watched Tolcet and Halsa ride up. There was a fire with a thin man stirring something in a pot. Two women were winding up a ball of rough-looking twine.

They were dressed like Tolcet. More wizards' servants, Halsa and Onion thought. Clearly wizards were very lazy.

"Down you go," Tolcet said, and Halsa gladly slid off the horse's back. Then Tolcet got down and lifted off the harness and the horse suddenly became a naked, brown girl of about fourteen years. She straightened her back and wiped her muddy hands on her legs. She didn't seem to care that she was naked. Halsa gaped at her.

The girl frowned. She said, "You be good, now, or they'll turn you into something even worse."

"Who?" Halsa said.

"The wizards of Perfil," the girl said, and laughed. It was a neighing, horsey laugh. All of the other children began to giggle.

"Oooh, Essa gave Tolcet a ride."

"Essa, did you bring me back a present?"

"Essa makes a prettier horse than she does a girl."

"Oh, shut up," Essa said. She picked up a rock and threw it. Halsa admired her economy of motion, and her accuracy.

"Oi!" her target said, putting her hand up to her ear. "That hurt, Essa."

"Thank you, Essa," Tolcet said. She made a remarkably graceful curtsy, considering that until a moment ago she had had four legs and no waist to speak of. There was a shirt and a pair of leggings folded and lying on a rock. Essa put them on. "This is Halsa," Tolcet said to the others. "I bought her in the market."

There was silence. Halsa's face was bright red. For once she was speechless. She looked at the ground and then up at the towers, and Onion looked, too, trying to catch a glimpse of a wizard. All the windows of the towers were empty, but he could feel the wizards of Perfil, feel the weight of their watching. The boggy ground under his feet was full of wizards' magic and the towers threw magic out like waves of heat from a stove. Magic clung even to the children and servants of the wizards of Perfil, as if they had been marinated in it.

"Come get something to eat," Tolcet said, and Halsa stumbled after him. There was a flat bread, and onions and fish. Halsa drank water that had the faint, slightly metallic taste of magic. Onion could taste it in his own mouth.

"Onion," someone said. "Bonti, Mik." Onion looked up. He was back in the market and his aunt stood there. "There's a church nearby where they'll let us sleep. The train leaves early tomorrow morning."

After she had eaten, Tolcet took Halsa into one of the towers, where there was a small cubby under the stairs. There was a pallet of reeds and a mothy wool blanket. The sun was still in the sky. Onion and his aunt and his cousins went to the church, where there was a yard where refugees might curl up and sleep a few hours. Halsa lay awake, thinking of the wizard in the room above the stairs where she was sleeping. The tower was so full of wizards' magic that she could hardly breathe. She imagined a wizard of Perfil creeping, creeping down the stairs above her cubby, and although the pallet was soft, she pinched her arms to stay awake. But Onion fell asleep immediately, as if drugged. He dreamed of wizards flying above the marshes like white lonely birds.

In the morning, Tolcet came and shook Halsa awake. "Go and fetch water for the wizard," he said. He was holding an empty bucket.

Halsa would have liked to say *go and fetch it yourself*, but she was not a stupid girl. She was a slave now. Onion was in her head again, telling her to be careful. "Oh, go away," Halsa said. She realized she had said this aloud, and flinched. But Tolcet only laughed.

Halsa rubbed her eyes and took the bucket and followed him. Outside, the air was full of biting bugs too small to see. They seemed to like the taste of Halsa. That seemed funny to Onion, for no reason that she could understand.

The other children were standing around the fire pit and eating porridge. "Are you hungry?" Tolcet said. Halsa nodded. "Bring the water up and then get yourself something to eat. It's not a good idea to keep a wizard waiting."

He led her along a well-trodden path that quickly sloped down into a small pool and disappeared. "The water is sweet here," he said. "Fill your bucket and bring it up to the top of the wizard's tower. I have an errand to run. I'll return before nightfall. Don't be afraid, Halsa."

"I'm not afraid," Halsa said. She knelt down and filled the bucket. She was almost back to the tower before she realized that the bucket was half empty again. There was a split in the wooden bottom. The other children were watching her and she straightened her back. *So it's a test,* she said in her head, to Onion.

You could ask them for a bucket without a hole in it, he said.

I don't need anyone's help, Halsa said. She went back down the path and scooped up a handful of clayey mud where the path ran into the pool. She packed this into the bottom of the bucket and then pressed moss down on top of the mud. This time the bucket held water.

There were three windows lined with red tiles on Halsa's wizard's tower, and a nest that some bird had built on an outcropping of stone. The roof was round and red and shaped like a bishop's hat. The stairs inside were narrow. The steps had been worn down, smooth and slippery as wax. The higher she went, the heavier the pail of water became. Finally she set it down on a step and sat down beside it. *Four hundred and twenty-two steps,* Onion said. Halsa had counted five hundred and ninety-eight. There seemed to be many more steps on the inside than one would have thought, looking at the tower from outside. "Wizardly tricks," Halsa said in disgust, as if she'd expected nothing better. "You would think they'd make it fewer steps rather than more steps. What's the use of more steps?"

When she stood and picked up the bucket, the handle broke in her hand. The water spilled down the steps and Halsa threw the bucket after it as hard as she could. Then she marched down the stairs and went to mend the bucket and fetch more water. It didn't do to keep wizards waiting.

At the top of the steps in the wizard's tower there was a door. Halsa set the bucket down and knocked. No one answered and so she knocked again. She tried the latch: the door was locked. Up here, the smell of magic was so thick that Halsa's eyes watered. She tried to look *through* the door. This is what she saw: a room, a window, a bed, a mirror, a table. The mirror was full of rushes and light and water. A bright-eyed fox was curled up on the bed, sleeping. A white bird flew through the unshuttered window, and then another and another. They circled around and around the room and then they began to mass on the table. One flung itself at the door where Halsa stood, peering in. She recoiled. The door vibrated with peck and blows.

She turned and ran down the stairs, leaving the bucket, leaving Onion behind her. There were even more steps on the way down. And there was no porridge left in the pot beside the fire.

Someone tapped her on the shoulder and she jumped. "Here," Essa said, handing her a piece of bread.

"Thanks," Halsa said. The bread was stale and hard. It was the most delicious thing she'd ever eaten.

"So your mother sold you," Essa said.

Halsa swallowed hard. It was strange, not being able to see inside Essa's head, but it was also restful. As if Essa might be anyone at all. As if Halsa herself might become anyone she wished to be. "I didn't care," she said. "Who sold you?"

"No one," Essa said. "I ran away from home. I didn't want to be a soldier's whore like my sisters."

"Are the wizards better than soldiers?" Halsa said.

Essa gave her a strange look. "What do you think? Did you meet your wizard?"

"He was old and ugly, of course," Halsa said. "I didn't like the way he looked at me."

Essa put her hand over her mouth as if she were trying not to laugh. "Oh dear," she said.

"What must I do?" Halsa said. "I've never been a wizard's servant before."

"Didn't your wizard tell you?" Essa said. "What did he tell you to do?"

Halsa blew out an irritated breath. "I asked what he needed, but he said nothing. I think he was hard of hearing."

Essa laughed long and hard, exactly like a horse, Halsa thought. There were three or four other children, now, watching them. They were all laughing at Halsa. "Admit it," Essa said. "You didn't talk to the wizard."

"So?" Halsa said. "I knocked, but no one answered. So obviously he's hard of hearing."

"Of course," a boy said.

"Or maybe the wizard is shy," said another boy. He had green eyes like Bonti and Mik. "Or asleep. Wizards like to take naps."

Everyone was laughing again.

"Stop making fun of me," Halsa said. She tried to look fierce and dangerous. Onion and her brothers would have quailed. "Tell me what my duties are. What does a wizard's servant do?"

Someone said, "You carry things up the stairs. Food. Firewood. Kaffa, when Tolcet brings it back from the market. Wizards like unusual things. Old things. So you go out in the marsh and look for things."

"Things?" Halsa said.

"Glass bottles," Essa said. "Petrified imps. Strange things, things out of the ordinary. Or ordinary things like plants or stones or animals or anything that feels right. Do you know what I mean?"

"No," Halsa said, but she did know. Some things felt more magic-soaked than other things. Her father had found an arrowhead in his field. He'd put it aside to take to the schoolmaster, but that night while everyone was sleeping, Halsa had wrapped it in a rag and taken it back to the field and buried it. Bonti got the blame. Sometimes Halsa wondered if that was what had brought the soldiers to kill her father, the malicious, evil luck of that arrowhead. But you couldn't blame a whole war on one arrowhead.

"Here," a boy said. "Go and catch fish if you're too stupid to know magic when you see it. Have you ever caught fish?"

Halsa took the fishing pole. "Take that path," Essa said. "The muddiest one. And stay on it. There's a pier out that way where the fishing is good."

When Halsa looked back at the wizards' towers, she thought she saw Onion looking down at her, out of a high window. But that was ridiculous. It was only a bird.

The train was so crowded that some passengers gave up and went and sat on top of the cars. Vendors sold umbrellas to keep the sun off. Onion's aunt had found two seats, and she and Onion sat with one twin on each lap. Two rich women sat across from them. You could tell they were rich because their shoes were green leather. They held filmy pink handkerchiefs like embroidered rose petals up to their rabbity noses. Bonti looked at them from under his eyelashes. Bonti was a terrible flirt.

Onion had never been on a train before. He could smell the furnace room of the train, rich with coal and magic. Passengers stumbled up and down the aisles, drinking and laughing as if they were at a festival. Men and women stood beside the train windows, sticking their heads in. They shouted messages. A woman leaning against the seats fell against Onion and Mik when someone shoved past her. "Pardon, sweet," she said, and smiled brilliantly. Her teeth were studded with gemstones. She was wearing at least four silk dresses, one on top of the other. A man across the aisle coughed wetly. There was a bandage wrapped around his throat, stained with red. Babies were crying.

"I hear they'll reach Perfil in three days or less," a man in the next row said.

"The king's men won't sack Perfil," said his companion. "They're coming to defend it."

"The king is mad," the man said. "God has told him all men are his enemies. He hasn't paid his army in two years. When they rebel, he just conscripts another army and sends them off to fight the first one. We're safer leaving."

"Oooh," a woman said, somewhere behind Onion. "At last we're off. Isn't this fun! What a pleasant outing!"

Onion tried to think of the marshes of Perfil, of the wizards. But Halsa was suddenly there on the train, instead. *You have to tell them,* she said.

Tell them what? Onion asked her, although he knew. When the train was in the mountains, there would be an explosion. There would be soldiers, riding down at the train. No one would reach Qual. *Nobody will believe me,* he said.

You should tell them anyway, Halsa said.

Onion's legs were falling asleep. He shifted Mik. *Why do you care?* he said. *You hate everyone.*

I don't! Halsa said. But she did. She hated her mother. Her mother had watched her husband die, and done nothing. Halsa had been screaming and her mother slapped her across the face. She hated the twins because they weren't like her, they didn't *see* things the way Halsa had to. Because they were little and they got tired and it had been so much work keeping them safe. Halsa had hated Onion, too, because he *was* like her. Because he'd been afraid of Halsa, and because the day he'd come to live with her family, she'd known that one day she would be like him, alone and without a family. Magic was bad luck, people like Onion and Halsa were bad luck. The only person who'd ever looked at Halsa and really seen her, really known her, had been Onion's mother. Onion's mother was kind and good and she'd known she was going to die. *Take care of my son,* she'd said to Halsa's mother and father, but she'd been looking at Halsa when she said it. But Onion would have to take care of himself. Halsa would make him.

Tell them, Halsa said. There was a fish jerking on her line. She ignored it. *Tell them, tell them, tell them.* She and Onion were in the marsh and on the train at the same time. Everything smelled like coal and salt and ferment. Onion ignored her the way she was ignoring the fish. He sat and dangled his feet in the water, even though he wasn't really there.

Halsa caught five fish. She cleaned them and wrapped them in leaves and brought them back to the cooking fire. She also brought back the greeny-copper key that had caught on her fishing line. "I found this," she said to Tolcet.

"Ah," Tolcet said. "May I see it?" It looked even smaller and more ordinary in Tolcet's hand.

"Burd," Tolcet said. "Where is the box you found, the one we couldn't open?"

The boy with green eyes got up and disappeared into one of the towers. He came out after a few minutes and gave Tolcet a metal box no bigger than a pickle jar. The key fit. Tolcet unlocked it, although it seemed to Halsa that she ought to have been the one to unlock it, not Tolcet.

"A doll," Halsa said, disappointed. But it was a strange-looking doll. It was carved out of a greasy black wood, and when Tolcet turned it over, it had no back, only two fronts, so it was always looking backward and forward at the same time.

"What do you think, Burd?" Tolcet said.

Burd shrugged. "It's not mine."

"It's yours," Tolcet said to Halsa. "Take it up the stairs and give it to your wizard. And refill the bucket with fresh water and bring some dinner, too. Did you think to take up lunch?"

"No," Halsa said. She hadn't had any lunch herself. She cooked the fish along with some greens Tolcet gave her, and ate two. The other three fish and the rest of the greens she carried up to the top of the stairs in the tower. She had to stop to rest twice, there were so many stairs this time. The door was still closed and the bucket on the top step was empty. She thought that maybe all the water had leaked away, slowly. But she left the fish and she went and drew more water and carried the bucket back up.

"I've brought you dinner," Halsa said, when she'd caught her breath. "And something else. Something I found in the marsh. Tolcet said I should give it to you."

Silence.

She felt silly, talking to the wizard's door. "It's a doll," she said. "Perhaps it's a magic doll."

Silence again. Not even Onion was there. She hadn't noticed when he went away. She thought of the train. "If I give you the doll," she said, "will you do something for me? You're a wizard, so you ought to be able to do anything, right? Will you help the people on the train? They're going to Qual. Something bad is going to happen if you won't stop it. You know about the soldiers? Can you stop them?"

Halsa waited for a long time, but the wizard behind the door never said anything. She put the doll down on the steps and then she picked it up again and put it in her pocket. She was furious. "I think you're a coward," she said. "That's why you hide up here, isn't it? I would have got on that train and I know what's going to happen. Onion got on that train. And you could stop it, but you won't. Well, if you won't stop it, then I won't give you the doll."

She spat in the bucket of water and then immediately wished she hadn't. "You keep the train safe," she said, "and I'll give you the doll. I promise. I'll bring you other things, too. And I'm sorry I spit in your water. I'll go and get more."

She took the bucket and went back down the stairs. Her legs ached and there were welts where the little biting bugs had drawn blood.

"Mud," Essa said. She was standing in the meadow, smoking a pipe. "The flies are only bad in the morning and at twilight. If you put mud on your face and arms, they leave you alone."

"It smells," Halsa said.

"So do you," Essa said. She snapped her clay pipe in two,

which seemed extravagant to Halsa, and wandered over to where some of the other children were playing a complicated-looking game of pickup sticks and dice. Under a night-flowering tree, Tolcet sat in a battered, oaken throne that looked as if it had been spat up by the marsh. He was smoking a pipe, too, with a clay stem even longer than Essa's had been. It was ridiculously long. "Did you give the poppet to the wizard?" he said.

"Oh yes," Halsa said.

"What did she say?"

"Well," Halsa said. "I'm not sure. She's young and quite lovely. But she had a horrible stutter. I could hardly understand her. I think she said something about the moon, how she wanted me to go cut her a slice of it. I'm to bake it into a pie."

"Wizards are very fond of pie," Tolcet said.

"Of course they are," Halsa said. "And I'm fond of my arse."

"Better watch your mouth," Burd, the boy with green eyes, said. He was standing on his head, for no good reason that Halsa could see. His legs waved in the air languidly, semaphoring. "Or the wizards will make you sorry."

"I'm already sorry," Halsa said. But she didn't say anything else. She carried the bucket of water up to the closed door. Then she ran back down the stairs to the cubbyhole and this time she fell straight asleep. She dreamed a fox came and looked at her. It stuck its muzzle in her face. Then it trotted up the stairs and ate the three fish Halsa had left there. *You'll be sorry,* Halsa thought. *The wizards will turn you into a one-legged crow.* But then she was chasing the fox up the aisle of a train to Qual, where her mother and her brothers and Onion were sleeping uncomfortably in their two seats, their legs tucked under them, their arms hanging down as if they were dead—the stink of coal and magic was even stronger than it had been in the morning. The train was laboring hard. It panted like a fox with a pack of dogs after it, dragging it-self along. There was no way it would reach all the way to the top of the wizard of Perfil's stairs. And if it did, the wizard wouldn't be there, anyway, just the moon, rising up over the mountains, round and fat as a lardy bone.

The wizards of Perfil don't write poetry, as a general rule. As far as anyone knows, they don't marry, or plow fields, or have much use for polite speech. It is said that the wizards of Perfil appreci-ate a good joke, but telling a joke to a wizard is dangerous busi-ness. What if the wizard doesn't find the joke funny? Wizards are sly, greedy, absentminded, obsessed with stars and bugs, parsimonious, frivolous, invisible, tyrannous, untrustworthy, se-cretive, inquisitive, meddlesome, long-lived, dangerous, useless, and have far too good an opinion of themselves. Kings go mad, the land is blighted, children starve or get sick or die spitted on the pointy end of a pike, and it's all beneath the notice of the wiz-ards of Perfil. The wizards of Perfil don't fight wars.

It was like having a stone in his shoe. Halsa was always there, nagging. *Tell them, tell them. Tell them.* They had been on the train for a day and a night. Halsa was in the swamp, getting farther and farther away. Why wouldn't she leave him alone? Mik and Bonti had seduced the two rich women who sat across from them. There were no more frowns or handkerchiefs, only smiles and tidbits of food and love, love, love all around. On went the train through burned fields and towns that had been put to the sword by one army or another. The train and its passengers overtook people on foot, or fleeing in wagons piled high with goods: mattresses, ward-robes, a pianoforte once, stoves and skillets and butter churns and pigs and angry-looking geese. Sometimes the train stopped while men got out and examined the tracks and made repairs. They did not stop at any stations, although there were people waiting, sometimes, who yelled and ran after the train. No one got off. There were fewer people up in the mountains, when they got there. Instead there was snow. Once Onion saw a wolf.

"When we get to Qual," one of the rich women, the older one, said to Onion's aunt, "my sister and I will set up our establishment. We'll need someone to keep house for us. Are you thrifty?" She had Bonti on her lap. He was half-asleep.

"Yes, ma'am," Onion's aunt said.

"Well, we'll see," said the woman. She was half in love with Bonti. Onion had never had much opportunity to see what the rich thought about. He was a little disappointed to find out that it was much the same as other people. The only difference seemed to be that the rich woman, like the wizard's secretary, seemed to think that all of this would end up all right. Money, it seemed, was like luck, or magic. All manner of things would be well, except they wouldn't. If it weren't for the thing that was going to happen to the train, perhaps Onion's aunt could have sold more of her children.

Why won't you tell them? Halsa said. *Soon it will be too late.*

You tell them, Onion thought back at her. Having an invisible Halsa around, always telling him things that he already knew, was far worse than the real Halsa had been. The real Halsa was safe, asleep, on the pallet under the wizard's stairs. Onion should have been there instead. Onion bet the wizards of Perfil were sorry that Tolcet had ever bought a girl like Halsa.

Halsa shoved past Onion. She put her invisible hands on her mother's shoulders and looked into her face. Her mother didn't look up. *You have to get off the train,* Halsa said. She yelled. *GET OFF THE TRAIN!*

But it was like talking to the door at the top of the wizard's tower. There was something in Halsa's pocket, pressing into her stomach so hard it almost felt like a bruise. Halsa wasn't on the train, she was sleeping on something with a sharp little face.

"Oh, stop yelling. Go away. How am I supposed to stop a train?" Onion said.

"Onion?" his aunt said. Onion realized he'd said it aloud. Halsa looked smug.

"Something bad is going to happen," Onion said, capitulating. "We have to stop the train and get off." The two rich women stared at him as if he were a lunatic. Onion's aunt patted his shoulder. "Onion," she said. "You were asleep. You were having a bad dream."

"But—" Onion protested.

"Here," his aunt said, glancing at the two women. "Take Mik for a walk. Shake off your dream."

Onion gave up. The rich women were thinking that perhaps they would be better off looking for a housekeeper in Qual. Halsa was tapping her foot, standing in the aisle with her arms folded.

Come on, she said. *No point talking to them. They just think you're crazy. Come talk to the conductor instead.*

"Sorry," Onion said to his aunt. "I had a bad dream. I'll go for a walk." He took Mik's hand.

They went up the aisle, stepping over sleeping people and people stupid or quarrelsome with drink, people slapping down playing cards. Halsa always in front of them: *Hurry up, hurry, hurry. We're almost there. You've left it too late. That useless wizard, I should have known not to bother asking for help. I should have known not to expect you to take care of things. You're as useless as they are. Stupid good-for-nothing wizards of Perfil.*

Up ahead of the train, Onion could feel the gunpowder

charges, little bundles wedged between the ties of the track. It was like there was a stone in his shoe. He wasn't afraid, he was merely irritated: at Halsa, at the people on the train who didn't even know enough to be afraid, at the wizards and the rich women who thought that they could just buy children, just like that. He was angry, too. He was angry at his parents, for dying, for leaving him stuck here. He was angry at the king, who had gone mad; at the soldiers, who wouldn't stay home with their own families, who went around stabbing and shooting and blowing up other people's families.

They were at the front of the train. Halsa led Onion right into the cab, where two men were throwing enormous scoops of coal into a red-black, boiling furnace. They were filthy as devils. Their arms bulged with muscles and their eyes were red. One turned and saw Onion. "Oi!" he said. "What's he doing here? You, kid, what are you doing?"

"You have to stop the train," Onion said. "Something is going to happen. I saw soldiers. They're going to make the train blow up."

"Soldiers? Back there? How long ago?"

"They're up ahead of us," Onion said. "We have to stop now."

Mik was looking up at him.

"He saw soldiers?" the other man said.

"Naw," said the first man. Onion could see he didn't know whether to be angry or whether to laugh. "The fucking kid's making things up. Pretending he sees things. Hey, maybe he's a wizard of Perfil! Lucky us, we got a wizard on the train!"

"I'm not a wizard," Onion said. Halsa snorted in agreement. "But I know things. If you don't stop the train, everyone will die."

Both men stared at him. Then the first said, angrily, "Get out of here, you. And don't go talking to people like that or we'll throw you in the boiler."

"Okay," Onion said "Come on, Mik."

Wait, Halsa said. *What are you doing? You have to make them understand. Do you want to be dead? Do you think you can prove something to me by being dead?*

Onion put Mik on his shoulders. *I'm sorry,* he said to Halsa. *But it's no good. Maybe you should just go away. Wake up. Catch fish. Fetch water for the wizards of Perfil.*

The pain in Halsa's stomach was sharper, as if someone were stabbing her. When she put her hand down, she had hold of the wooden doll.

What's that? Onion said.

Nothing, Halsa said. *Something I found in the swamp. I said I would give it to the wizard, but I won't! Here, you take it!*

She thrust it at Onion. It went all the way through him. It was an uncomfortable feeling, even though it wasn't really there. *Halsa,* he said. He put Mik down.

Take it! she said. *Here! Take it now!*

The train was roaring. Onion knew where they were; he recognized the way the light looked. Someone was telling a joke in the front of the train, and in a minute a woman would laugh. It would be a lot brighter in a minute. He put his hand up to stop the thing that Halsa was stabbing him with and something smacked against his palm. His fingers brushed Halsa's fingers.

It was a wooden doll with a sharp little nose. There was a nose on the back of its head, too. *Oh, take it!* Halsa said. Something was pouring out of her, through the doll, into Onion. Onion fell back against a woman holding a birdcage on her lap. "Get off!" the woman said. It *hurt.* The stuff pouring out of Halsa felt like *life*, as if the doll were pulling out her life like a skein of heavy, sodden, black wool. It hurt Onion, too. Black stuff poured and poured through the doll, into him, until there was no space for Onion, no space to breathe or think or see. The black stuff welled up in his throat, pressed behind his eyes. "Halsa," he said, "let go!"

The woman with the birdcage said, "What's wrong with him?"

Mik said, "What's wrong? What's wrong?"

The light changed. *Onion*, Halsa said, and let go of the doll. He staggered backward. The tracks beneath the train were singing *tara-ta tara-ta ta-rata-ta*. Onion's nose was full of swamp water and coal and metal and magic. "No," Onion said. He threw the doll at the woman holding the birdcage and pushed Mik down on the floor. "No," Onion said again, louder. People were staring at him. The woman who'd been laughing at the joke had stopped laughing. Onion covered Mik with his body. The light grew brighter and blacker, all at once.

Onion! Halsa said. But she couldn't see him anymore. She was awake in the cubby beneath the stair. The doll was gone.

Halsa had seen men coming home from the war. Some of them had been blinded. Some had lost a hand or an arm. She'd seen one man wrapped in lengths of cloth and propped up in a dog cart that his young daughter pulled on a rope. He'd had no legs, no arms. When people looked at him, he cursed them. There was another man who ran a cockpit in Larch. He came back from the war and paid a man to carve him a leg out of knotty pine. At first he was unsteady on the pine leg, trying to find his balance again. It had been funny to watch him chase after his cocks, like watching a windup toy. By the time the army came through Larch again, though, he could run as fast as anyone.

It felt as if half of her had died on the train in the mountains. Her ears rang. She couldn't find her balance. It was as if a part of her had been cut away, as if she were blind. The part of her that *knew* things, *saw* things, wasn't there anymore. She went about all day in a miserable deafening fog.

She brought water up the stairs and she put mud on her arms and legs. She caught fish, because Onion had said that she ought to catch fish. Late in the afternoon, she looked and saw Tolcet sitting beside her on the pier.

"You shouldn't have bought me," she said. "You should have bought Onion. He wanted to come with you. I'm bad-tempered and unkind and I have no good opinion of the wizards of Perfil."

"Of whom do you have a low opinion? Yourself or the wizards of Perfil?" Tolcet asked.

"How can you serve them?" Halsa said. "How can you serve men and women who hide in towers and do nothing to help people who need help? What good is magic if it doesn't serve anyone?"

"These are dangerous times," Tolcet said. "For wizards as well as for children."

"Dangerous times! Hard times! Bad times," Halsa said. "Things have been bad since the day I was born. Why do I see things and know things, when there's nothing I can do to stop them? When will there be better times?"

"What do you see?" Tolcet said. He took Halsa's chin in his hand and tilted her head this way and that, as if her head were a glass ball that he could see inside. He put his hand on her head and smoothed her hair as if she were his own child. Halsa closed her eyes. Misery welled up inside her.

"I don't see anything," she said. "It feels like someone wrapped me in a wool blanket and beat me and left me in the dark. Is this what it feels like not to see anything? Did the wizards of Perfil do this to me?"

"Is it better or worse?" Tolcet said.

"Worse," Halsa said. "No. Better. I don't know. What am I to do? What am I to be?"

"You are a servant of the wizards of Perfil," Tolcet said. "Be patient. All things may yet be well."

Halsa said nothing. What was there to say?

She climbed up and down the stairs of the wizard's tower, carrying water, toasted bread and cheese, little things that she found in the swamp. The door at the top of the stairs was never open. She couldn't see through it. No one spoke to her, although she sat there sometimes, holding her breath so that the wizard would think she had gone away again. But the wizard wouldn't be fooled so easily. Tolcet went up the stairs, too, and perhaps the wizard admitted him. Halsa didn't know.

Essa and Burd and the other children were kind to her, as if they knew that she had been broken. She knew that she wouldn't have been kind to them if their situations had been reversed. But perhaps they knew that, too. The two women and the skinny man kept their distance. She didn't even know their names. They disappeared on errands and came back again and disappeared into the towers.

Once, when she was coming back from the pier with a bucket of fish, there was a dragon on the path. It wasn't very big, only the size of a mastiff. But it gazed at her with wicked, jeweled eyes. She couldn't get past it. It would eat her, and that would be that. It was almost a relief. She put the bucket down and stood waiting to be eaten. But then Essa was there, holding a stick. She hit the dragon on its head, once, twice, and then gave it a kick for good measure. "Go on, you!" Essa said. The dragon went, giving Halsa one last reproachful look. Essa picked up the bucket of fish. "You have to be firm with them," she said. "Otherwise they get inside your head and make you feel as if you deserve to be eaten. They're too lazy to eat anything that puts up a fight."

Halsa shook off a last, wistful regret, almost sorry not to have been eaten. It was like waking up from a dream, something beautiful and noble and sad and utterly untrue. "Thank you," she said to Essa. Her knees were trembling.

"The bigger ones stay away from the meadow," Essa said. "It's the smaller ones who get curious about the wizards of Perfil. And by 'curious,' what I really mean is hungry. Dragons eat the things that they're curious about. Come on, let's go for a swim."

Sometimes Essa or one of the others would tell Halsa stories about the wizards of Perfil. Most of the stories were silly, or plainly untrue. The children sounded almost indulgent, as if they found their masters more amusing than frightful. There were other stories, sad stories about long-ago wizards who had fought great battles or gone on long journeys. Wizards who had perished by treachery or been imprisoned by ones they'd thought friends.

Tolcet carved her a comb. Halsa found frogs whose backs were marked with strange mathematical formulas, and put them in a bucket and took them to the top of the tower. She caught a mole with eyes like pinpricks and a nose like a fleshy pink hand. She found the hilt of a sword, a coin with a hole in it, the outgrown carapace of a dragon, small as a badger and almost weightless, but hard, too. When she cleaned off the mud that covered it, it shone dully, like a candlestick. She took all of these up the stairs. She couldn't tell whether the things she found had any meaning. But she took a small, private pleasure in finding them nevertheless.

The mole had come back down the stairs again, fast, wriggly, and furtive. The frogs were still in the bucket, making their gloomy pronouncements, when she returned with the wizard's dinner. But other things disappeared behind the wizard of Perfil's door.

The thing that Tolcet had called Halsa's gift came back, a little at a time. Once again, she became aware of the wizards in their towers, and of how they watched her. There was something else, too. It sat beside her, sometimes, while she was fishing, or when she rowed out in the abandoned coracle Tolcet helped her to repair. She thought she knew who, or what, it was. It was the part of Onion that he'd learned to send out. It was what was left of him: shadowy, thin, and silent. It wouldn't talk to her. It only watched. At night, it stood beside her pallet and watched her sleep. She was glad it was there. To be haunted was a kind of comfort.

She helped Tolcet repair a part of the wizard's tower where the stones were loose in their mortar. She learned how to make paper out of rushes and bark. Apparently wizards needed a great deal of paper. Tolcet began to teach her how to read.

One afternoon when she came back from fishing, all of the wizards' servants were standing in a circle. There was a leveret motionless as a stone in the middle of the circle. Onion's ghost crouched down with the other children. So Halsa stood and watched, too. Something was pouring back and forth between the leveret and the servants of the wizards of Perfil. It was the same as it had been for Halsa and Onion, when she'd given him the two-faced doll. The leveret's sides rose and fell.

Its eyes were glassy and dark and knowing. Its fur bristled with magic.

"Who is it?" Halsa said to Burd. "Is it a wizard of Perfil?"

"Who?" Burd said. He didn't take his eyes off the leveret. "No, not a wizard. It's a hare. Just a hare. It came out of the marsh."

"But," Halsa said. "But I can feel it. I can almost hear what it's saying."

Burd looked at her. Essa looked too. "Everything speaks," he said, speaking slowly, as if to a child. "Listen, Halsa."

There was something about the way Burd and Essa were looking at her, as if it were an invitation, as if they were asking her to look inside their heads, to see what they were thinking. The others were watching, too, watching Halsa now, instead of the leveret. Halsa took a step back. "I can't," she said. "I can't hear anything."

She went to fetch water. When she came out of the tower, Burd and Essa and the other children weren't there. Leverets dashed between towers, leaping over one another, tussling in midair. Onion sat on Tolcet's throne, watching and laughing silently. She didn't think she'd seen Onion laugh since the death of his mother. It made her feel strange to know that a dead boy could be so joyful.

The next day Halsa found an injured fox kit in the briar. It snapped at her when she tried to free it and the briars tore her hand. There was a tear in its belly and she could see a shiny gray loop of intestine. She tore off a piece of her shirt and wrapped it around the fox kit. She put the kit in her pocket. She ran all the way back to the wizard's tower, all the way up the steps. She didn't count them. She didn't stop to rest. Onion followed her, quick as a shadow.

When she reached the door at the top of the stairs, she knocked hard. No one answered.

"Wizard!" she said.

No one answered.

"Please help me," she said. She lifted the fox kit out of her pocket and sat down on the steps with it swaddled in her lap. It didn't try to bite her. It needed all its energy for dying. Onion sat next to her. He stroked the kit's throat.

"Please," Halsa said again. "Please don't let it die. Please do something."

She could feel the wizard of Perfil, standing next to the door. The wizard put a hand out, as if—at last—the door might open. She saw that the wizard loved foxes and all the wild marsh things. But the wizard said nothing. The wizard didn't love Halsa. The door didn't open.

"Help me," Halsa said one more time. She felt that dreadful black pull again, just as it had been on the train with Onion. It was as if the wizard were yanking at her shoulder, shaking her in a stony, black rage. How dare someone like Halsa ask a wizard for help. Onion was shaking her, too. Where Onion's hand gripped her, Halsa could feel stuff pouring through her and out of her. She could feel the kit, feel the place where its stomach had torn open. She could feel its heart pumping blood, its panic and fear and the life that was spilling out of it. Magic flowed up and down the stairs of the tower. The wizard of Perfil was winding it up like a skein of black, tarry wool, and then letting it go again. It poured through Halsa and Onion and the fox kit until Halsa thought she would die.

"Please," she said, and what she meant this time was *stop*. It would kill her. And then she was empty again. The magic had gone through her and there was nothing left of it or her. Her bones had been turned into jelly. The fox kit began to struggle, clawing at her. When she unwrapped it, it sank its teeth into her wrist and then ran down the stairs as if it had never been dying at all.

Halsa stood up. Onion was gone, but she could still feel the wizard standing there on the other side of the door. "Thank you," she said. She followed the fox kit down the stairs.

The next morning she woke and found Onion lying on the pallet beside her. He seemed nearer, somehow, this time. As if he weren't entirely dead. Halsa felt that if she tried to speak to him, he would answer. But she was afraid of what he would say.

Essa saw Onion too. "You have a shadow," she said.

"His name is Onion," Halsa said.

"Help me with this," Essa said. Someone had cut lengths of bamboo. Essa was fixing them in the ground, using a mixture of rocks and mud to keep them upright. Burd and some of the other children wove rushes through the bamboo, making walls, Halsa saw.

"What are we doing?" Halsa asked.

"There is an army coming," Burd said. "To burn down the town of Perfil. Tolcet went to warn them."

"What will happen?" Halsa said. "Will the wizards protect the town?"

Essa laid another bamboo pole across the tops of the two upright poles. She said, "They can come to the marshes, if they want to, and take refuge. The army won't come here. They're afraid of the wizards."

"Afraid of the wizards!" Halsa said. "Why? The wizards are cowards and fools. Why won't they save Perfil?"

"Go ask them yourself," Essa said. "If you're brave enough."

"Halsa?" Onion said. Halsa looked away from Essa's steady

gaze. For a moment there were two Onions. One was the shadowy ghost from the train, close enough to touch. The second Onion stood beside the cooking fire. He was filthy, skinny, and real. Shadow-Onion guttered and then was gone.

"Onion?" Halsa said.

"I came out of the mountains," Onion said. "Five days ago, I think. I didn't know where I was going, except that I could see you. Here. I walked and walked and you were with me and I was with you."

"Where are Mik and Bonti?" Halsa said. "Where's Mother?"

"There were two women on the train with us. They were rich. They've promised to take care of Mik and Bonti. They will. I know they will. They were going to Qual. When you gave me the doll, Halsa, you saved the train. We could see the explosion, but we passed through it. The tracks were destroyed and there were clouds and clouds of black smoke and fire, but nothing touched the train. We saved everyone."

"Where's Mother?" Halsa said again. But she already knew. Onion was silent. The train stopped beside a narrow stream to take on water. There was an ambush. Soldiers. There was a bottle with water leaking out of it. Halsa's mother had dropped it. There was an arrow sticking out of her back.

Onion said, "I'm sorry, Halsa. Everyone was afraid of me, because of how the train had been saved. Because I knew that there was going to be an explosion. Because I didn't know about the ambush and people died. So I got off the train."

"Here," Burd said to Onion. He gave him a bowl of porridge. "No, eat it slowly. There's plenty more."

Onion said with his mouth full, "Where are the wizards of Perfil?"

Halsa began to laugh. She laughed until her sides ached and

until Onion stared at her and until Essa came over and shook her. "We don't have time for this," Essa said. "Take that boy and find him somewhere to lie down. He's exhausted."

"Come on," Halsa said to Onion. "You can sleep in my bed. Or if you'd rather, you can go knock on the door at the top of the tower and ask the wizard of Perfil if you can have his bed."

She showed Onion the cubby under the stairs and he lay down on it. "You're dirty," she said. "You'll get the sheets dirty."

"I'm sorry," Onion said.

"It's fine," Halsa said. "We can wash them later. There's plenty of water here. Are you still hungry? Do you need anything?"

"I brought something for you," Onion said. He held out his hand and there were the earrings that had belonged to his mother.

"No," Halsa said.

Halsa hated herself. She was scratching at her own arm, ferociously, not as if she had an insect bite, but as if she wanted to dig beneath the skin. Onion saw something that he hadn't known before, something astonishing and terrible, that Halsa was no kinder to herself than to anyone else. No wonder Halsa had wanted the earrings—just like the snakes, Halsa would gnaw on herself if there was nothing else to gnaw on. How Halsa wished that she'd been kind to her mother.

Onion said, "Take them. Your mother was kind to me, Halsa. So I want to give them to you. My mother would have wanted you to have them, too."

"All right," Halsa said. She wanted to weep, but she scratched and scratched instead. Her arm was white and red from scratching. She took the earrings and put them in her pocket. "Go to sleep now."

"I came here because you were here," Onion said. "I wanted to tell you what had happened. What should I do now?"

"Sleep," Halsa said.

"Will you tell the wizards that I'm here? How we saved the train?" Onion said. He yawned so wide that Halsa thought his head would split in two. "Can I be a servant of the wizards of Perfil?"

"We'll see," Halsa said. "You go to sleep. I'll go climb the stairs and tell them that you've come."

"It's funny," Onion said. "I can feel them all around us. I'm glad you're here. I feel safe."

Halsa sat on the bed. She didn't know what to do. Onion was quiet for a while and then he said, "Halsa?"

"What?" Halsa said.

"I can't sleep," he said, apologetically.

"Shhh," Halsa said. She stroked his filthy hair. She sang a song her father had liked to sing. She held Onion's hand until his breathing became slower and she was sure that he was sleeping. Then she went up the stairs to tell the wizard about Onion. "I don't understand you," she said to the door. "Why do you hide away from the world? Don't you get tired of hiding?"

The wizard didn't say anything.

"Onion is braver than you are," Halsa told the door. "Essa is braver. My mother was—"

She swallowed and said, "She was braver than you. Stop ignoring me. What good are you, up here? You won't talk to me, and you won't help the town of Perfil, and Onion's going to be very disappointed when he realizes that all you do is skulk around in your room, waiting for someone to bring you breakfast. If you like waiting so much, then you can wait as long as you like. I'm not going to bring you any food or any water or anything that I find in the swamp. If you want anything, you can magic it. Or you can come get it yourself. Or you can turn me into a toad."

She waited to see if the wizard would turn her into a toad. "All right," she said at last. "Well, good-bye then." She went back down the stairs.

The wizards of Perfil are lazy and useless. They hate to climb stairs and they never listen when you talk. They don't answer questions because their ears are full of beetles and wax and their faces are wrinkled and hideous. Marsh fairies live deep in the wrinkles of the faces of the wizards of Perfil and the marsh fairies ride around in the bottomless canyons of the wrinkles on saddle-broken fleas who grow fat grazing on magical, wizardly blood. The wizards of Perfil spend all night scratching their fleabites and sleep all day. I'd rather be a scullery maid than a servant of the invisible, doddering, nearly blind, flea-bitten, mildewy, clammy-fingered, conceited marsh-wizards of Perfil.

Halsa checked Onion, to make sure that he was still asleep. Then she went and found Essa. "Will you pierce my ears for me?" she said.

Essa shrugged. "It will hurt," she said.

"Good," said Halsa. So Essa boiled water and put her needle in it. Then she pierced Halsa's ears. It did hurt, and Halsa was glad. She put on Onion's mother's earrings, and then she helped Essa and the others dig latrines for the townspeople of Perfil.

Tolcet came back before sunset. There were half a dozen women and their children with him.

"Where are the others?" Essa said.

Tolcet said, "Some don't believe me. They don't trust wizardly folk. There are some that want to stay and defend the town. Others are striking out on foot for Qual, along the tracks."

"Where is the army now?" Burd said.

"Close," Halsa said. Tolcet nodded.

The women from the town had brought food and bedding. They seemed subdued and anxious, and it was hard to tell whether it was the approaching army or the wizards of Perfil that scared them most. The women stared at the ground. They didn't look up at the towers. If they caught their children looking up, they scolded them in low voices.

"Don't be silly," Halsa said crossly to a woman whose child had been digging a hole near a tumbled tower. The woman shook him until he cried and cried and wouldn't stop. What was she thinking? That wizards liked to eat mucky children who dug holes? "The wizards are lazy and unsociable and harmless. They keep to themselves and don't bother anyone."

The woman only stared at Halsa, and Halsa realized that she was as afraid of Halsa as she was of the wizards of Perfil. Halsa was amazed. Was she that terrible? Mik and Bonti and Onion had always been afraid of her, but they'd had good reason to be. And she'd changed. She was as mild and meek as butter now.

Tolcet, who was helping with dinner, snorted as if he'd caught her thought. The woman grabbed up her child and rushed away, as if Halsa might open her mouth again and eat them both.

"Halsa, look." It was Onion, awake and so filthy that you could smell him from two yards away. They would need to burn his clothes. Joy poured through Halsa, because Onion had come to find her and because he was here and because he was alive. He'd come out of Halsa's tower, where he'd gotten her cubby bed grimy and smelly, how wonderful to think of it, and he was pointing east, toward the town of Perfil. There was a red glow hanging over the marsh, as if the sun were rising instead of setting. Everyone was silent, looking east as if they might be able to see what was happening in Perfil. Presently the wind carried an ashy, desolate smoke over the marsh. "The war has come to Perfil," a woman said.

"Which army is it?" another woman said, as if the first woman might know.

"Does it matter?" said the first woman. "They're all the same. My eldest went off to join the king's army and my youngest joined General Balder's men. They've set fire to plenty of towns, and killed other mothers' sons and maybe one day they'll kill each other, and never think of me. What difference does it make to the town that's being attacked, to know what army is attacking them? Does it matter to a cow who kills her?"

"They'll follow us," someone else said in a resigned voice. "They'll find us here and they'll kill us all!"

"They won't," Tolcet said. He spoke loudly. His voice was calm and reassuring. "They won't follow you and they won't find you here. Be brave for your children. All will be well."

"Oh, please," Halsa said, under her breath. She stood and glared up at the towers of the wizards of Perfil, her hands on her hips. But as usual, the wizards of Perfil were up to nothing. They didn't strike her dead for glaring. They didn't stand at their windows to look out over the marshes to see the town of Perfil and how it was burning while they only stood and watched. Perhaps they were already asleep in their beds, dreaming about breakfast, lunch, and dinner. She went and helped Burd and Essa and the others make up beds for the refugees from Perfil. Onion cut up wild onions for the stew pot. He was going to have to have a bath soon, Halsa thought. Clearly he needed someone like Halsa to tell him what to do.

None of the servants of the wizards of Perfil slept. There was too much work to do. The latrines weren't finished. A child wandered off into the marshes and had to be found before it drowned or met a dragon. A little girl fell into the well and had to be hauled up.

Before the sun came up again, more refugees from the town of Perfil arrived. They came into the camp in groups of twos or threes, until there were almost a hundred townspeople in the wizards' meadow. Some of the newcomers were wounded or badly burned or deep in shock. Essa and Tolcet took charge. There were compresses to apply, clothes that had already been cut up for bandages, hot drinks that smelled bitter and medicinal and not particularly magical. People went rushing around, trying to discover news of family members or friends who had stayed behind. Young children who had been asleep woke up and began to cry.

"They put the mayor and his wife to the sword," a man was saying.

"They'll march on the king's city next," an old woman said. "But our army will stop them."

"It *was* our army—I saw the butcher's boy and Philpot's middle son. They said that we'd been trading with the enemies of our country. The king sent them. It was to teach us a lesson. They burned down the market church and they hung the pastor from the bell tower."

There was a girl lying on the ground who looked Mik and Bonti's age. Her face was gray. Tolcet touched her stomach lightly and she emitted a thin, high scream, not a human noise at all, Onion thought. The marshes were so noisy with magic that he couldn't hear what she was thinking, and he was glad.

"What happened?" Tolcet said to the man who'd carried her into the camp.

"She fell," the man said. "She was trampled underfoot."

Onion watched the girl, breathing slowly and steadily, as if he could somehow breathe for her. Halsa watched Onion. Then: "That's enough," she said. "Come on, Onion."

She marched away from Tolcet and the girl, shoving through the refugees.

"Where are we going?" Onion said.

"To make the wizards come down," Halsa said. "I'm sick and tired of doing all their work for them. Their cooking and fetching. I'm going to knock down that stupid door. I'm going to drag them down their stupid stairs. I'm going to make them help that girl."

There were a lot of stairs this time. Of course the accursed wizards of Perfil would know what she was up to. This was their favorite kind of wizardly joke, making her climb and climb and climb. They'd wait until she and Onion got to the top and then they'd turn them into lizards. Well, maybe it wouldn't be so bad, being a small poisonous lizard. She could slip under the door and bite one of the damned wizards of Perfil. She went up and up and up, half running and half stumbling, until it seemed she and Onion must have climbed right up into the sky. When the stairs abruptly ended, she was still running. She crashed into the door so hard that she saw stars.

"Halsa?" Onion said. He bent over her. He looked so worried that she almost laughed.

"I'm fine," she said. "Just wizards playing tricks." She hammered on the door, then kicked it for good measure. "Open up!"

"What are you doing?" Onion said.

"It never does any good," Halsa said. "I should have brought an ax."

"Let me try," Onion said.

Halsa shrugged. *Stupid boy*, she thought, and Onion could hear her perfectly. "Go ahead," she said.

Onion put his hand on the door and pushed. It swung open. He looked up at Halsa and flinched. "Sorry," he said.

Halsa went in.

There was a desk in the room, and a single candle, which was burning. There was a bed, neatly made, and a mirror on the wall over the desk. There was no wizard of Perfil, not even hiding under the bed. Halsa checked, just in case.

She went to the empty window and looked out. There was the meadow and the makeshift camp, below them, and the marsh. The canals, shining like silver. There was the sun, coming up, the way it always did. It was strange to see all the windows of the other towers from up here, so far above, all empty. White birds were floating over the marsh. She wondered if they were wizards; she wished she had a bow and arrows.

"Where is the wizard?" Onion said. He poked the bed. Maybe the wizard had turned himself into a bed. Or the desk. Maybe the wizard was a desk.

"There are no wizards," Halsa said.

"But I can feel them!" Onion sniffed, then sniffed harder. He could practically smell the wizard, as if the wizard of Perfil had turned himself into a mist or a vapor that Onion was inhaling. He sneezed violently.

Someone was coming up the stairs. He and Halsa waited to see if it was a wizard of Perfil. But it was only Tolcet. He looked tired and cross, as if he'd had to climb many, many stairs.

"Where are the wizards of Perfil?" Halsa said.

Tolcet held up a finger. "A minute to catch my breath," he said.

Halsa stamped her foot. Onion sat down on the bed. He apologized to it silently, just in case it was the wizard. Or maybe the candle was the wizard. He wondered what happened if you tried to blow a wizard out. Halsa was so angry he thought she might explode.

Tolcet sat down on the bed beside Onion. "A long time ago," he said, "the father of the present king visited the wizards of Perfil. He'd had certain dreams about his son, who was only a baby. He was afraid of these dreams. The wizards told him that he was right to be afraid. His son would go mad. There would be war and famine and more war and his son would be to blame. The old king went into a rage. He sent his men to throw the wizards of Perfil down from their towers. They did."

"Wait," Onion said. "Wait. What happened to the wizards? Did they turn into white birds and fly away?"

"No," Tolcet said. "The king's men slit their throats and threw them out of the towers. I was away. When I came back, the towers had been ransacked. The wizards were dead."

"No!" Halsa said. "Why are you lying? I know the wizards are here. They're hiding somehow. They're cowards."

"I can feel them too," Onion said.

"Come and see," Tolcet said. He went to the window. When they looked down, they saw Essa and the other servants of the wizards of Perfil moving among the refugees. The two old women who never spoke were sorting through bundles of clothes and blankets. The thin man was staking down someone's cow. Children were chasing chickens as Burd held open the gate of a makeshift pen. One of the younger girls, Perla, was singing a lullaby to some mother's baby. Her voice, rough and sweet at the same time, rose straight up to the window of the tower, where Halsa and Onion and Tolcet stood looking down. It was a song they all knew. It was a song that said all would be well.

"Don't you understand?" Tolcet, the wizard of Perfil, said to Halsa and Onion. "There are the wizards of Perfil. They are young, most of them. They haven't come into their full powers yet. But all may yet be well."

"Essa is a wizard of Perfil?" Halsa said. Essa, a shovel in her hand, looked up at the tower, as if she'd heard Halsa. She smiled and shrugged, as if to say, *Perhaps I am, perhaps not, but isn't it a good joke? Didn't you ever wonder?*

Tolcet turned Halsa and Onion around so that they faced the mirror that hung on the wall. He rested his strong, speckled hands on their shoulders for a minute, as if to give them courage. Then he pointed to the mirror, to the reflected Halsa and Onion who stood there staring back at themselves, astonished. Tolcet began to laugh. Despite everything, he laughed so hard that tears came from his eyes. He snorted. Onion and Halsa began to laugh, too. They couldn't help it. The wizard's room was full of magic, and so were the marshes and Tolcet and the mirror where the children and Tolcet stood reflected, and the children were full of magic, too.

Tolcet pointed again at the mirror, and his reflection pointed its finger straight back at Halsa and Onion. Tolcet said, "Here they are in front of you! Ha! Do you know them? Here are the wizards of Perfil!"

It's night in The Free People's World-Tree Library.
All the librarians are asleep, tucked into their coffins, their
scabbards, priest-holes, button holes, pockets, hidden cupboards, between the pages of their enchanted novels.

MAGIC FOR BEGINNERS

FOX IS A television character, and she isn't dead yet. But she will be, soon. She's a character on a television show called *The Library*. You've never seen *The Library* on TV, but I bet you wish you had.

In one episode of *The Library*, a boy named Jeremy Mars, fifteen years old, sits on the roof of his house in Plantagenet, Vermont. It's eight o'clock at night, a school night, and he and his friend Elizabeth should be studying for the math quiz which their teacher, Mr. Cliff, has been hinting at all week long. Instead, they've sneaked out onto the roof. It's cold. They don't know everything they should know about X, when X is the square root of Y. They don't even know Y. They ought to go in.

But there's nothing good on TV and the sky is very beautiful. They have jackets on, and up in the corners where the sky begins are patches of white in the darkness, still, where there's snow, up on the mountains. Down in the trees around the house, some animal is making a small, anxious sound: "Why cry? Why cry?"

"What's that one?" Elizabeth says, pointing at a squarish configuration of stars.

"That's The Parking Structure," Jeremy says. "And right next to that is The Big Shopping Mall and The Lesser Shopping Mall."

"And that's Orion, right? Orion the Bargain Hunter?"

Jeremy squints up. "No, Orion is over there. That's The Austrian Bodybuilder. That thing that's sort of wrapped around his lower leg is The Amorous Cephalopod. The Hungry, Hungry Octopus. It can't make up its mind whether it should eat him or make crazy, eight-legged love to him. You know that myth, right?"

"Of course," Elizabeth says. "Is Karl going to be pissed off that we didn't invite him over to study?"

"Karl's always pissed off about something," Jeremy says. Jeremy is resolutely resisting a notion about Elizabeth. Why are they sitting up here? Was it his idea or was it hers? Are they friends, are they just two friends sitting on the roof and talking? Or is Jeremy supposed to try to kiss her? He thinks maybe he's supposed to kiss her. If he kisses her, will they still be friends? He can't ask Karl about this. Karl doesn't believe in being helpful. Karl believes in mocking.

Jeremy doesn't even know if he wants to kiss Elizabeth. He's never thought about it until right now.

"I should go home," Elizabeth says. "There could be a new episode on right now, and we wouldn't even know."

"Someone would call and tell us," Jeremy says. "My mom would come up and yell for us." His mother is something else Jeremy doesn't want to worry about, but he does, he does.

Jeremy Mars knows a lot about the planet Mars, although he's never been there. He knows some girls, and yet he doesn't know much about them. He wishes there were books about girls, the way there are books about Mars, that you could observe the orbits and brightness of girls through telescopes without appearing to be perverted. Once Jeremy read a book about Mars out loud to Karl, except he kept replacing the word Mars with the word "girls." ("It was in the seventeenth century that girls at last came under serious scrutiny." "Girls have virtually no surface liquid water: their temperatures are too cold and the air is too thin." And so on.) Karl cracked up every time.

Jeremy's mother is a librarian. His father writes books. Jeremy reads biographies. He plays trombone in a marching band. He jumps hurdles while wearing a school tracksuit. Jeremy is also passionately addicted to a television show in which a renegade librarian and magician named Fox is trying to save her world from thieves, murderers, cabalists, and pirates. Jeremy is a geek, although he's a telegenic geek. Somebody should make a TV show about him.

Jeremy's friends call him Germ, although he would rather be called Mars. His parents haven't spoken to each other in a week.

Jeremy doesn't kiss Elizabeth. The stars don't fall out of the sky, and Jeremy and Elizabeth don't fall off the roof either. They go inside and finish their homework.

Someone that Jeremy has never met, never even heard of—a woman named Cleo Baldrick—has died. Lots of people, so far, have managed to live and die without making the acquaintance of Jeremy Mars, but Cleo Baldrick has left Jeremy Mars and his mother something strange in her will: a phone booth on a state highway, some forty miles outside of Las Vegas, and a Las Vegas wedding chapel. The wedding chapel is called Hell's Bells. Jeremy isn't sure what kind of people get married there. Bikers, maybe. Supervillains, freaks, and Satanists.

Jeremy's mother wants to tell him something. It's probably something about Las Vegas and about Cleo Baldrick, who—it turns out—was his mother's great-aunt. (Jeremy never knew his mother had a great-aunt. His mother is a mysterious person.) But it may be, on the other hand, something concerning Jeremy's father. For a week and a half now, Jeremy has managed to avoid finding out what his mother is worrying about. It's easy not to find out things, if you try hard enough. There's band practice. He has overslept on weekdays in order to rule out conversations at breakfast, and at night he climbs up on the roof with his telescope to look at stars, to look at Mars. His mother is afraid of heights. She grew up in L.A.

It's clear that whatever it is she has to tell Jeremy is not something she wants to tell him. As long as he avoids being alone with her, he's safe.

But it's hard to keep your guard up at all times. Jeremy comes home from school, feeling as if he has passed the math test, after all. Jeremy is an optimist. Maybe there's something good on TV. He settles down with the remote control on one of his father's pet couches: oversized and reupholstered in an orange-juice-colored corduroy that makes it appear as if the couch has just escaped from a maximum security prison for criminally insane furniture. This couch looks as if its hobby is devouring interior decorators. Jeremy's father is a horror writer, so no one should be surprised if some of the couches he reupholsters are hideous and eldritch.

Jeremy's mother comes into the room and stands above the couch, looking down at him. "Germ?" she says. She looks absolutely miserable, which is more or less how she has looked all week.

The phone rings and Jeremy jumps up.

As soon as he hears Elizabeth's voice, he knows. She says, "Germ, it's on. Channel forty-two. I'm taping it." She hangs up.

"It's on!" Jeremy says. "Channel forty-two! Now!"

His mother has the television on by the time he sits down. Being a librarian, she has a particular fondness for *The Library*. "I should go tell your dad," she says, but instead she sits down beside Jeremy. And of course it's now all the more clear something is wrong between Jeremy's parents. But *The Library* is on and Fox is about to rescue Prince Wing.

When the episode ends, he can tell without looking over that his mother is crying. "Don't mind me," she says and wipes her nose on her sleeve. "Do you think she's really dead?"

But Jeremy can't stay around and talk.

Jeremy has always wondered about what kind of television shows the characters *in* television shows watch. Television characters almost always have better haircuts, funnier friends, simpler attitudes toward sex. They marry magicians, win lotteries, have affairs with women who carry guns in their purses. Curious things happen to them on an hourly basis. Jeremy and I can forgive their haircuts. We just want to ask them about their television shows.

Just like always, it's Elizabeth who worked out in the nick of time that the new episode was on. Everyone will show up at Elizabeth's house afterwards, for the postmortem. This time, it really is a postmortem. Why did Prince Wing kill Fox? How could Fox let him do it? Fox is ten times stronger.

Jeremy runs all the way, slapping his old track shoes against the sidewalk for the pleasure of the jar, for the sweetness of the sting. He likes the rough, cottony ache in his lungs. His coach says you have to be part masochist to enjoy something like running. It's nothing to be ashamed of. It's something to exploit.

Talis opens the door. She grins at him, although he can tell that she's been crying, too. She's wearing a T-shirt that says I'M SO GOTH I SHIT TINY VAMPIRES.

"Hey," Jeremy says. Talis nods. Talis isn't so Goth, at least not as far as Jeremy or anyone else knows. Talis just has a lot of T-shirts. She's an enigma wrapped in a mysterious T-shirt. A woman once said to Calvin Coolidge, "Mr. President, I bet my husband that I could get you to say more than two words." Coolidge said, "You lose." Jeremy can imagine Talis as Calvin Coolidge in a former life. Or maybe she was one of those dogs that don't bark. A basenji. Or a rock. A dolmen. There was an episode of *The Library*, once, with some sinister dancing dolmens in it.

Elizabeth comes up behind Talis. If Talis is unGoth, then Elizabeth is Ballerina Goth. She likes hearts and skulls and black pen-ink tattoos, pink tulle and Hello Kitty. When the woman who invented Hello Kitty was asked why Hello Kitty was so popular, she said, "Because she has no mouth." Elizabeth's mouth is small. Her lips are chapped.

"That was the most horrible episode ever! I cried and cried," she says. "Hey, Germ, so I was telling Talis about how you inherited a gas station."

"A phone booth," Jeremy says. "In Las Vegas. This great-great aunt died. And there's a wedding chapel, too."

"Hey! Germ!" Karl says, yelling from the living room. "Shut up and get in here! The commercial with the talking cats is on—"

"Shut it, Karl," Jeremy says. He goes in and sits on Karl's head. You have to show Karl who's boss once in a while.

Amy turns up last. She was in the next town over, buying comics. She hasn't seen the new episode and so they all shut it (except for Talis, who has not been saying anything at all), and Elizabeth puts on the tape.

In the previous episode of *The Library*, masked pirate-magicians said they would sell Prince Wing a cure for the spell which infested Faithful Margaret's hair with miniature, wicked, fire-breathing golems. (Faithful Margaret's hair keeps catching fire, but she refuses to shave it off. Her hair is the source of all her magic.)

The pirate-magicians lured Prince Wing into a trap so obvious that it seemed impossible it could really be a trap, on the one-hundred-and-fortieth floor of The Free People's World-Tree Library. The pirate-magicians used finger magic to turn Prince Wing into a porcelain teapot, put two Earl Grey tea bags into the teapot, and poured in boiling water, toasted the Eternally Postponed and Overdue Reign of the Forbidden Books, drained their tea in one gulp, belched, hurled their souvenir pirate mugs to the ground, and then shattered the teapot which had been Prince Wing into hundreds of pieces. Then the wicked pirate-magicians swept the pieces of both Prince Wing and the collectible mugs carelessly into a wooden cigar box, buried the box in the Angela Carter Memorial Park on the seventeenth floor of The World-Tree Library, and erected a statue of George Washington above it.

So then Fox had to go looking for Prince Wing. When she finally discovered the park on the seventeenth floor of

The Library, the George Washington statue stepped down off his plinth and fought her tooth and nail. Literally tooth and nail, and they'd all agreed that there was something especially nightmarish about a biting, scratching, life-sized statue of George Washington with long, pointed metal fangs that threw off sparks when he gnashed them. The statue of George Washington bit Fox's pinky finger right off, just like Gollum biting Frodo's finger off on the top of Mount Doom. But of course, once the statue tasted Fox's magical blood, it fell in love with Fox. It would be her ally from now on.

In the new episode, the actor playing Fox is a young Latina actress whom Jeremy Mars thinks he recognizes. She has been a snotty but well-intentioned fourth-floor librarian in an episode about an epidemic of food-poisoning that triggered bouts of invisibility and/or levitation, and she was also a lovelorn, suicidal Bear Cult priestess in the episode where Prince Wing discovered his mother was one of the Forbidden Books.

This is one of the best things about *The Library*, the way the cast swaps parts, all except for Faithful Margaret and Prince Wing, who are only ever themselves. Faithful Margaret and Prince Wing are the love interests and the main characters, and therefore, inevitably, the most boring characters, although Amy has a crush on Prince Wing.

Fox and the dashing-but-treacherous pirate-magician Two Devils are never played by the same actor twice, although in the twenty-third episode of *The Library*, the same woman played them both. Jeremy supposes that the casting could be perpetually confusing, but instead it makes your brain catch on fire. It's magical.

You always know Fox by her costume (the too-small green T-shirt, the long, full skirts she wears to hide her tail), by her dramatic hand gestures and body language, by the soft, breathy-squeaky voice the actors use when they are Fox. Fox is funny, dangerous, bad-tempered, flirtatious, greedy, untidy, accident-prone, graceful, and has a mysterious past. In some episodes, Fox is played by male actors, but she always sounds like Fox. And she's always beautiful. Every episode you think that this Fox, surely, is the most beautiful Fox there could ever be, and yet the Fox of the next episode will be even more heartbreakingly beautiful.

On television, it's night in The Free People's World-Tree Library. All the librarians are asleep, tucked into their coffins, their scabbards, priest-holes, button holes, pockets, hidden cupboards, between the pages of their enchanted novels. Moonlight pours through the high, arched windows of The Library and between the aisles of shelves, into the park. Fox is on her knees, clawing at the muddy ground with her bare hands. The statue of George Washington kneels beside her, helping.

"So that's Fox, right?" Amy says. Nobody tells her to shut up. It would be pointless. Amy has a large heart and an even larger mouth. When it rains, Amy rescues worms off the sidewalk. When you get tired of having a secret, you tell Amy.

Understand: Amy isn't that much stupider than anyone else in this story. It's just that she thinks out loud.

Elizabeth's mother comes into the living room. "Hey, guys," she says. "Hi, Jeremy. Did I hear something about your mother inheriting a wedding chapel?"

"Yes, ma'am," Jeremy says. "In Las Vegas."

"Las Vegas," Elizabeth's mom says. "I won three hundred bucks once in Las Vegas. Spent it on a helicopter ride over the Grand Canyon. So how many times can you guys watch the same episode in one day?" But she sits down to watch, too. "Do you think she's really dead?"

"Who's dead?" Amy says. Nobody says anything.

Jeremy isn't sure he's ready to see this episode again so soon, anyway, especially not with Amy. He goes upstairs and takes a shower. Elizabeth's family has a large and distracting selection of shampoos. They don't mind when Jeremy uses their bathroom.

Jeremy and Karl and Elizabeth have known each other since the first day of kindergarten. Amy and Talis are a year younger. The five have not always been friends, except for Jeremy and Karl, who have. Talis is, famously, a loner. She doesn't listen to music as far as anyone knows, she doesn't wear significant amounts of black, she isn't particularly good (or bad) at math or English, and she doesn't drink, debate, knit, or refuse to eat meat. If she keeps a blog, she's never admitted it to anyone.

The Library made Jeremy and Karl and Talis and Elizabeth and Amy friends. No one else in school is as passionately devoted. Besides, they are all the children of former hippies, and the town is small. They all live within a few blocks of each other, in run-down Victorians with high ceilings and ranch houses with sunken living rooms. And although they have not always been friends, growing up, they've gone skinny-dipping in lakes on summer nights, and broken bones on each others' trampolines. Once, during an argument about dog names, Elizabeth, who is hot-tempered, tried to run Jeremy over with her ten-speed bicycle, and once, a year ago, Karl got drunk on green-apple schnapps at a party and tried to kiss Talis, and once, for five months in the seventh grade, Karl and Jeremy communicated only through angry e-mails written in all caps. I'm not allowed to tell you what they fought about.

Now the five are inseparable; invincible. They imagine that

life will always be like this—like a television show in eternal syndication—that they will always have each other. They use the same vocabulary. They borrow each other's books and music. They share lunches, and they never say anything when Jeremy comes over and takes a shower. They all know Jeremy's father is eccentric. He's supposed to be eccentric. He's a novelist.

When Jeremy comes back downstairs, Amy is saying, "I've always thought there was something wicked about Prince Wing. He's a dork and he looks like he has bad breath. I never really liked him."

Karl says, "We don't know the whole story yet. Maybe he found out something about Fox while he was a teapot." Elizabeth's mom says, "He's under a spell. I bet you anything." They'll be talking about it all week.

Talis is in the kitchen, making a Velveeta-and-pickle sandwich.

"So what did you think?" Jeremy says. It's like having a hobby, only more pointless, trying to get Talis to talk. "Is Fox really dead?"

"Don't know," Talis says. Then she says, "I had a dream."

Jeremy waits. Talis seems to be waiting, too. She says, "About you." Then she's silent again. There is something dreamlike about the way that she makes a sandwich. As if she is really making something that isn't a sandwich at all; as if she's making something far more meaningful and mysterious. Or as if soon he will wake up and realize that there is no such thing as sandwiches.

"You and Fox," Talis says. "The dream was about the two of you. She told me. To tell you. To call her. She gave me a phone number. She was in trouble. She said you were in trouble. She said *to keep in touch*."

"Weird," Jeremy says, mulling this over. He's never had a dream about *The Library*. He wonders who was playing Fox in Talis's dream. He had a dream about Talis, once, but it isn't the kind of dream that you'd ever tell anybody about. They were just sitting together, not saying anything. Even Talis's T-shirt hadn't said anything. Talis was holding his hand.

"It didn't feel like a dream," Talis says.

"So what was the phone number?" Jeremy says.

"I forgot," Talis says. "When I woke up, I forgot."

Kurt's mother works in a bank. Talis's father has a karaoke machine in his basement, and he knows all the lyrics to "Like a Virgin" and "Holiday" as well as the lyrics to all the songs from *Godspell* and *Cabaret*. Talis's mother is a licensed therapist who composes multiple-choice personality tests for women's magazines. "Discover Which Television Character You Resemble Most." Etc. Amy's parents met in a commune in Ithaca: her name was Galadriel Moon Shuyler before her parents came to their senses and had it changed legally. Everyone is sworn to secrecy about this, which is ironic, considering that this is Amy.

But Jeremy's father is Gordon Strangle Mars. He writes novels about giant spiders, giant leeches, giant moths, and once, notably, a giant carnivorous rosebush who lives in a mansion in upstate New York, and falls in love with a plucky, teenaged girl with a heart murmur. Saint Bernard–sized spiders chase his characters' cars down dark, bumpy country roads. They fight the spiders off with badminton rackets, lawn tools, and fireworks. The novels with spiders are all bestsellers.

Once a Gordon Strangle Mars fan broke into the Mars house. The fan stole several German first editions of Gordon

Strangle's novels, a hairbrush, and a used mug in which there were two ancient, dehydrated tea bags. The fan left behind a betrayed and abusive letter on a series of Post-It notes, and the manuscript of his own novel, told from the point of view of the iceberg that sank the *Titanic*. Jeremy and his mother read the manuscript out loud to each other. It begins: "The iceberg knew it had a destiny." Jeremy's favorite bit happens when the iceberg sees the doomed ship drawing nearer, and remarks plaintively, "Oh my, does not the Captain know about my large and impenetrable bottom?"

Jeremy discovered, later, that the novel-writing fan had put Gordon Strangle Mars's used tea bags and hairbrush up for sale on eBay, where someone paid forty-two dollars and sixty-eight cents, which was not only deeply creepy, but, Jeremy still feels, somewhat cheap. But of course this is appropriate, as Jeremy's father is famously stingy and just plain weird about money.

Gordon Strangle Mars once spent eight thousand dollars on a Japanese singing toilet. Jeremy's friends love that toilet. Jeremy's mother has a painting of a woman wearing a red dress by some artist, Jeremy can never remember who. Jeremy's father gave her that painting. The woman is beautiful, and she looks right at you as if you're the painting, not her. As if *you're* beautiful. The woman has an apple in one hand and a knife in the other. When Jeremy was little, he used to dream about eating that apple. Apparently it's worth more than the whole house and everything else in the house combined, including the singing toilet. But art and toilets aside, the Marses buy most of their clothes at thrift stores.

Jeremy's father clips coupons.

On the other hand, when Jeremy was twelve and begged

his parents to send him to baseball camp in Florida, his father ponied up. And on Jeremy's last birthday, his father gave him a couch reupholstered in several dozen yards of heavy-duty *Star Wars*–themed fabric. That was a good birthday.

When his writing is going well, Gordon Strangle Mars likes to wake up at 6 A.M. and go out driving. He works out new plot lines about giant spiders and keeps an eye out for abandoned couches, which he wrestles into the back of his pickup truck. Then he writes for the rest of the day. On weekends he reupholsters the thrown-away couches in remaindered, discount fabrics. A few years ago, Jeremy went through his house, counting up fourteen couches, eight love seats, and one rickety chaise longue. That was a few years ago. Once Jeremy had a dream that his father combined his two careers and began reupholstering giant spiders.

All lights in all rooms of the Mars house are on fifteen-minute timers, in case Jeremy or his mother leaves a room and forgets to turn off a lamp. This has caused confusion—and sometimes panic—on the rare occasions that the Marses throw dinner parties.

Everyone thinks that writers are rich, but it seems to Jeremy that his family is only rich some of the time. Some of the time they aren't.

Whenever Gordon Mars gets stuck in a Gordon Strangle Mars novel, he worries about money. He worries that he won't, in fact, manage to finish the current novel. He worries that it will be terrible. He worries that no one will buy it and no one will read it, and that the readers who do read it will demand to be refunded the cost of the book. He's told Jeremy that he imagines these angry readers marching on the Mars house, carrying torches and crowbars.

It would be easier on Jeremy and his mother if Gordon Mars

did not work at home. It's difficult to shower when you know your father is timing you, and thinking dark thoughts about the water bill, instead of concentrating on the scene in the current Gordon Strangle Mars novel, in which the giant spiders have returned to their old haunts in the trees surrounding the ninth hole of the accursed golf course, where they sullenly feast on the pulped entrail-juices of a brace of unlucky poodles and their owner.

During these periods, Jeremy showers at school, after gym, or at his friends' houses, even though it makes his mother unhappy. She says that sometimes you just need to ignore Jeremy's father. She takes especially long showers, lots of baths. She claims that baths are even nicer when you know that Jeremy's father is worried about the water bill. Jeremy's mother has a cruel streak.

What Jeremy likes about showers is the way you can stand there, surrounded by water and yet in absolutely no danger of drowning, and not think about things like whether you fucked up on the Spanish assignment, or why your mother is looking so worried. Instead you can think about things like if there's water on Mars, and whether or not Karl is shaving, and if so, who is he trying to fool, and what the statue of George Washington meant when it said to Fox, during their desperate, bloody fight, "You have a long journey ahead of you," and, "Everything depends on this." And is Fox really dead?

After she dug up the cigar box, and after George Washington helped her carefully separate out the pieces of tea mug from the pieces of teapot, after they glued back together the hundreds of pieces of porcelain, when Fox turned the ramshackle teapot back into Prince Wing, Prince Wing looked about a hundred years old, and as if maybe there were still a few pieces missing. He looked pale. When he saw Fox, he turned even paler, as if he hadn't expected her to be standing there in front of him. He picked up his leviathan sword, which Fox had been keeping safe for him—the one which faithful viewers know was carved out of the tooth of a giant, ancient sea creature that lived happily and peacefully (before Prince Wing was tricked into killing it) in the enchanted underground sea on the third floor—and skewered the statue of George Washington like a kebab, pinning it to a tree. He kicked Fox in the head, knocked her down, and tied her to a card catalog. He stuffed a handful of moss and dirt into her mouth so she couldn't say anything, and then he accused her of plotting to murder Faithful Margaret by magic. He said Fox was more deceitful than a Forbidden Book. He cut off Fox's tail and her ears and he ran her through with the poison-edged, dog-headed knife that he and Fox had stolen from his mother's secret house. Then he left Fox there, tied to the card catalog, limp and bloody, her beautiful head hanging down. He sneezed (Prince Wing is allergic to swordplay) and walked off into the stacks. The librarians crept out of their hiding places. They untied Fox and cleaned off her face. They held a mirror to her mouth, but the mirror stayed clear and unclouded.

When the librarians pulled Prince Wing's leviathan sword out of the tree, the statue of George Washington staggered over and picked up Fox in his arms. He tucked her ears and tail into the capacious pockets of his bird-shit-stained, verdigris riding coat. He carried Fox down seventeen flights of stairs, past the enchanted-and-disagreeable Sphinx on the eighth floor, past the enchanted-and-stormy underground sea on the third floor, past the even-more-enchanted checkout desk on the first floor, and through the hammered-brass doors of the Free People's World-Tree Library. Nobody in *The Library*, not in one single episode, has ever gone outside. *The Library* is full of all the sorts of things that one usually has to go outside to enjoy: trees and lakes and grottoes and fields and mountains and precipices (and full of indoors things as well, like books, of course). Outside The Library, everything is dusty and red and alien, as if George Washington has carried Fox out of The Library and onto the surface of Mars.

"I could really go for a nice cold Euphoria right now," Jeremy says. He and Karl are walking home.

Euphoria is *The Librarian's Tonic—When Watchfulness Is Not Enough*. There are frequently commercials for Euphoria on *The Library*. Although no one is exactly sure what Euphoria is for, whether it is alcoholic or caffeinated, what it tastes like, if it is poisonous or delightful, or even whether or not it's carbonated, everyone, including Jeremy, pines for a glass of Euphoria once in a while.

"Can I ask you a question?" Karl says.

"Why do you always say that?" Jeremy says. "What am I going to say? 'No, you can't ask me a question'?"

"What's up with you and Talis?" Karl says. "What were you talking about in the kitchen?" Jeremy sees that Karl has been Watchful.

"She had this dream about me," he says, uneasily.

"So do you like her?" Karl says. His chin looks raw. Jeremy is sure now that Karl has tried to shave. "Because, remember how I liked her first?"

"We were just talking," Jeremy says. "So did you shave? Because I didn't know you had facial hair. The idea of you shaving is pathetic, Karl. It's like voting Republican if we were old enough to vote. Or farting in Music Appreciation."

"Don't try to change the subject," Karl says. "When have you and Talis ever had a conversation before?"

"One time we talked about a Diana Wynne Jones book that

she'd checked out from the library. She dropped it in the bath accidentally. She wanted to know if I could tell my mother," Jeremy says. "Once we talked about recycling."

"Shut up, Germ," Karl says. "Besides, what about Elizabeth? I thought you liked Elizabeth!"

"Who said that?" Jeremy says. Karl is glaring at him.

"Amy told me," Karl says.

"I never told Amy I liked Elizabeth," Jeremy says. So now Amy is a mind-reader as well as a blabbermouth? What a terrible, deadly combination!

"No," Karl says, grudgingly. "Elizabeth told Amy that she likes you. So I just figured you liked her back."

"Elizabeth likes me?" Jeremy says.

"Apparently everybody likes you," Karl says. He sounds sorry for himself. "What is it about you? It's not like you're all that special. Your nose is funny looking and you have stupid hair."

"Thanks, Karl." Jeremy changes the subject. "Do you think Fox is really dead?" he says. "For good?" He walks faster, so that Karl has to almost-jog to keep up. Presently Jeremy is much taller than Karl, and he intends to enjoy this as long as it lasts. Knowing Karl, he'll either get tall, too, or else chop Jeremy off at the knees.

"They'll use magic," Karl says. "Or maybe it was all a dream. They'll make her alive again. I'll never forgive them if they've killed Fox. And if you like Talis, I'll never forgive you, either. And I know what you're thinking. You're thinking that I think I mean what I say, but if push came to shove, eventually I'd forgive you, and we'd be friends again, like in seventh grade. But I wouldn't, and you're wrong, and we wouldn't be. We wouldn't ever be friends again."

Jeremy doesn't say anything. Of course he likes Talis. He

just hasn't realized how much he likes her, until recently. Until today. Until Karl opened his mouth. Jeremy likes Elizabeth, too, but how can you compare Elizabeth and Talis? You can't. Elizabeth is Elizabeth and Talis is Talis.

"When you tried to kiss Talis, she hit you with a boa constrictor," he says. It had been Amy's boa constrictor. It had probably been an accident. Karl shouldn't have tried to kiss someone while she was holding a boa constrictor.

"Just try to remember what I just said," Karl says. "You're free to like anyone you want to. Anyone except for Talis."

The Library has been on television for two years now. It isn't a regularly scheduled program. Sometimes it's on two times in the same week, and then not on again for another couple of weeks. Often new episodes debut in the middle of the night. There is a large online community who spend hours scanning channels, sending out alarms and false alarms; fans swap theories, tapes, files, write fanfic. Elizabeth has rigged up her computer to shout "Wake up, Elizabeth! The television is on fire!" when reliable *Library*-watch sites discover a new episode.

The Library is a pirate TV show. It's shown up once or twice on most network channels, but usually it's on the kind of channels that Jeremy thinks of as ghost channels. The ones that are just static, unless you're paying for several hundred channels of cable. There are commercial breaks, but the products being advertised are like Euphoria. They never seem to be real brands or things that you can actually buy. Often the commercials aren't even in English, or in any other identifiable language, although the jingles are catchy, nonsense or not. They get stuck in your head.

Episodes of *The Library* have no regular schedule, no credits, and sometimes not even dialogue. One episode of *The Library* takes place inside the top drawer of a card catalog, in pitch dark, and it's all in Morse code with subtitles. Nothing else. No one has ever claimed responsibility for inventing *The Library*. No one has ever interviewed one of the actors, or stumbled across a set, film crew, or script, although in one documentary-style episode, the actors filmed the crew, who all wore paper bags on their heads.

When Jeremy gets home, his father is making upside-down pizza in a casserole dish for dinner.

Meeting writers is usually disappointing, at best. Writers who write sexy thrillers aren't necessarily sexy or thrilling in person. Children's book writers might look more like accountants, or ax murderers for that matter. Horror writers are very rarely scary looking, although they are frequently good cooks.

Though Gordon Strangle Mars *is* scary looking. He has long, thin fingers—currently slimy with pizza sauce—which is why he chose "Strangle" for his fake middle name. He has white-blond hair that he tugs on while he writes until it stands straight up. He has a bad habit of suddenly appearing beside you when you haven't even realized he was in the same part of the house. His eyes are deep-set and he doesn't blink very often. Karl says that when you meet Jeremy's father, he looks at you as if he were imagining you bundled up and stuck away in some giant spider's larder. Which is probably true.

People who read books probably never bother to wonder if their favorite writers are also good parents. Why would they?

Gordon Strangle Mars is a recreational shoplifter. He has a special, complicated, and unspoken arrangement with the local bookstore, where, in exchange for his autographing as many

Gordon Strangle Mars novels as they can possibly sell, the store allows Jeremy's father to shoplift books and doesn't call the police. Jeremy's mother shows up sooner or later and writes a check.

Jeremy's feelings about his father are complicated. His father is a cheapskate and a petty thief, and yet Jeremy likes his father. His father hardly ever loses his temper with Jeremy, he is always interested in Jeremy's life, and he gives interesting (if confusing) advice when Jeremy asks for it. For example, if Jeremy asked his father about kissing Elizabeth, his father might suggest that Jeremy not worry about giant spiders when he kisses Elizabeth. Jeremy's father's advice usually has something to do with giant spiders.

When Jeremy and Karl weren't speaking to each other, it was Jeremy's father who straightened them out. He lured Karl over, and then locked them both into his study. He didn't let them out again until they were on speaking terms.

"I thought of a great idea for your book," Jeremy says. "What if one of the spiders builds a web on a soccer field, across a goal? And what if the goalie doesn't notice until the middle of the game? Could somebody kill one of the spiders with a soccer ball, if they kicked it hard enough? Would it explode? Or even better, the spider could puncture the soccer ball with its massive fangs. That would be cool, too."

"Your mother's out in the garage," Gordon Strangle Mars says to Jeremy. "She wants to talk to you."

"Oh," Jeremy says. All of a sudden, he thinks of Fox in Talis's dream, trying to phone him. Trying to warn him. Unreasonably, he feels that it's his parents' fault that Fox is dead now, as if they have killed her. "Is it about you? Are you getting divorced?"

"I don't know," his father says. He hunches his shoulders. He makes a face. It's a face that Jeremy's father makes frequently, and yet this face is even more pitiful and guilty than usual.

"What did you do?" Jeremy says. "Did you get caught shop-lifting at Wal-Mart?"

"No," his father says.

"Did you have an affair?"

"No!" his father says, again. Now he looks disgusted, either with himself or with Jeremy for asking such a horrible question. "I screwed up. Let's leave it at that."

"How's the book coming?" Jeremy says. There is something in his father's voice that makes him feel like kicking something, but there are never giant spiders around when you need them.

"I don't want to talk about that, either," his father says, looking, if possible, even more ashamed. "Go tell your mother dinner will be ready in five minutes. Maybe you and I can watch the new episode of *The Library* after dinner, if you haven't already seen it a thousand times."

"Do you know the end? Did Mom tell you that Fox is—"

"Oh shit," his father interrupts. "They killed Fox?"

That's the problem with being a writer, Jeremy knows. Even the biggest and most startling twists are rarely twists for you. You know how every story goes.

Jeremy's mother is an orphan. Jeremy's father claims that she was raised by feral silent-film stars, and it's true, she looks like a heroine out of a Harold Lloyd movie. She has an appealingly disheveled look to her, as if someone has either just tied her to or untied her from a set of train tracks. She met Gordon Mars (before he added the Strangle and sold his first novel) in the food court of a mall in New Jersey, and fell in love with him before realizing that he was a writer and a recreational shoplifter. She didn't read anything he'd written until after they were married, which was a typically cunning move on Jeremy's father's part.

Jeremy's mother doesn't read horror novels. She doesn't like ghost stories or unexplained phenomena or even the kind of phenomena that require excessively technical explanations. For example: microwaves, airplanes. She doesn't like Halloween, not even Halloween candy. Jeremy's father gives her special editions of his novels, where the scary pages have been glued together.

Jeremy's mother is quiet more often than not. Her name is Alice and sometimes Jeremy thinks about how the two quietest people he knows are named Alice and Talis. But his mother and Talis are quiet in different ways. Jeremy's mother is the kind of person who seems to be keeping something hidden, something secret. Whereas Talis just *is* a secret. Jeremy's mother could easily turn out to be a secret agent. But Talis is the death ray or the key to immortality or whatever it is that secret agents have to keep secret. Hanging out with Talis is like hanging out with a teenaged black hole.

Jeremy's mother is sitting on the floor of the garage, beside a large cardboard box. She has a photo album in her hands. Jeremy sits down beside her.

There are photographs of a cat on a wall, and something blurry that looks like a whale or a zeppelin or a loaf of bread. There's a photograph of a small girl sitting beside a woman. The woman wears a fur collar with a sharp little muzzle, four legs, and a tail, and Jeremy feels a sudden pang. Fox is the first dead person that he's ever cared about, but she's not real. The little girl in the photograph looks utterly blank, as if someone has just hit her with a hammer. Like the person behind the camera has just said, "Smile! Your parents are dead!"

"Cleo," Jeremy's mother says, pointing to the woman. "That's Cleo. She was my mother's aunt. She lived in Los Angeles. I went to live with her when my parents died. I was four. I know I've never talked about her. I've never really known what to say about her."

Jeremy says, "Was she nice?"

His mother says, "She tried to be nice. She didn't expect to be saddled with a little girl. What an odd word. Saddled. As if she were a horse. As if somebody put me on her back and I never got off again. She liked to buy clothes for me. She liked clothes. She hadn't had a happy life. She drank a lot. She liked to go to movies in the afternoon and to séances in the evenings. She had boyfriends. Some of them were jerks. The love of her life was a small-time gangster. He died and she never married. She always said marriage was a joke and that life was a bigger joke, and it was just her bad luck that she didn't have a sense of humor. So it's strange to think that all these years she was running a wedding chapel."

Jeremy looks at his mother. She's half-smiling, half-grimacing, as if her stomach hurts. "I ran away when I was sixteen. And I never saw her again. Once she sent me a letter, care of your father's publishers. She said she'd read all his books, and that was how she found me, I guess, because he kept dedicating them to me. She said she hoped I was happy and that she thought about me. I wrote back. I sent a photograph of you. But she never wrote again. Sounds like an episode of *The Library*, doesn't it?"

Jeremy says, "Is that what you wanted to tell me? Dad said you wanted to tell me something."

"That's part of it," his mother says. "I have to go out to Las Vegas, to check out some things about this wedding chapel. Hell's Bells. I want you to come with me."

"Is that what you wanted to ask me?" Jeremy says, although he knows there's something else. His mother still has that sad half-smile on her face.

"Germ," his mother says. "You know I love your father, right?"

"Why?" Jeremy says. "What did he do?"

His mother flips through the photo album. "Look," she says. "This was when you were born." In the picture, his father holds Jeremy as if someone has just handed him an enchanted porcelain teapot. Jeremy's father grins, but he looks terrified, too. He looks like a kid. A scary, scared kid.

"He wouldn't tell me either," Jeremy says. "So it has to be pretty bad. If you're getting divorced, I think you should go ahead and tell me."

"We're not getting divorced," his mother says, "but it might be a good thing if you and I went out to Las Vegas. We could stay there for a few months while I sort out this inheritance. Take care of Cleo's estate. I'm going to talk to your teachers. I've given notice at the library. Think of it as an adventure."

She sees the look on Jeremy's face. "No, I'm sorry. That was a stupid, stupid thing to say. I know this isn't an adventure."

"I don't want to go," Jeremy says. "All my friends are here! I can't just go away and leave them. That would be terrible!" All this time, he's been preparing himself for the most terrible thing he can imagine. He's imagined a conversation with his mother in which his mother reveals her terrible secret, and in his imagination, he's been calm and reasonable. His imaginary parents have wept and asked for his understanding. The imaginary Jeremy has understood. He has imagined himself understanding everything. But now, as his mother talks, Jeremy's heartbeat speeds up, and his lungs fill with air, as if he is running. He starts to sweat, although the floor of the garage is cold. He wishes he were sitting up on top of the roof with his telescope. There could be meteors, invisible to the naked eye, careening through the sky, hurtling toward Earth. Fox is dead. Everyone he knows is doomed. Even as he thinks this, he knows he's overreacting. But it doesn't help to know this.

"I know it's terrible," his mother says. His mother knows something about terrible.

"So why can't I stay here?" Jeremy says. "You go sort things out in Las Vegas, and I'll stay here with Dad. Why can't I stay here?"

"Because he put you in a book!" his mother says. She spits the words out. He has never heard her sound so angry. His mother never gets angry. "He put you in one of his books! I was in his office, and the manuscript was on his desk. I saw your name, and so I picked it up and started reading."

"So what?" Jeremy says. "He's put me in his books before. Like, stuff I've said. Like when I was eight and I was running a fever and told him the trees were full of dead people wearing party hats. Like when I accidentally set fire to his office."

"It isn't like that," his mother says. "He hasn't even changed your name. The boy in the book, he jumps hurdles and he wants to be a rocket scientist and go to Mars, and he's cute and funny and sweet and his best friend Elizabeth is in love with him and he talks like you and he looks like you and then he dies, Jeremy. He has a brain tumor and he dies. He dies. There aren't any giant spiders. There's just you, and you die."

Jeremy is silent. He imagines his father writing the scene in his book where the kid named Jeremy dies, and crying, just a little. He imagines this Jeremy kid, Jeremy the character who dies. Poor messed-up kid. Now Jeremy and Fox have something in common. They're both made-up people. They're both dead.

"Elizabeth is in love with me?" he says. Just on principle, he never believes anything that Karl says. But if it's in a book, maybe it's true.

"Oh shit," his mother says. "I really didn't want to say that. I'm just so angry at him. We've been married for seventeen years. I was just four years older than you when I met him, Jeremy. I was nineteen. He was only twenty. We were babies. Can you imagine that? I can put up with the singing toilet and the shoplifting and the couches, and I can put up with him being so weird about money. But he killed you, Jeremy. He wrote you into a book and he killed you off. And he knows it was wrong, too. He's ashamed of himself. He didn't want me to tell you. I didn't mean to tell you."

Jeremy sits and thinks. "I still don't want to go to Las Vegas," he says to his mother. "Maybe we could send Dad there instead."

His mother says, "Not a bad idea." But he can tell she's already planning their itinerary.

In one episode of *The Library*, everyone was invisible. You couldn't see the actors: you could only see the books and the bookshelves and the study carrels on the fifth floor where the coin-operated wizards come to flirt and practice their spells. Invisible Forbidden Books were fighting invisible pirate-magicians and the pirate-magicians were fighting Fox and her friends, who were also invisible. The fight was clumsy and full of deadly accidents. You could hear them fighting. Shelves were overturned. Books were thrown. Invisible people tripped over invisible dead bodies, but you didn't find out who'd died until the next episode. Several of the characters—The Accidental Sword, Hairy Pete, and

Ptolemy Krill, who (much like the Vogons in Douglas Adams's *The Hitchhiker's Guide to the Galaxy*) wrote poetry so bad it killed anyone who read it—disappeared for good, and nobody is sure whether they're dead or not.

In another episode, Fox stole a magical drug from The Norns, a prophetic girl band who headline at a cabaret on the mezzanine of The Free People's World-Tree Library. She accidentally injected it, became pregnant, and gave birth to a bunch of snakes who led her to the exact shelf where renegade librarians had misshelved an ancient and terrible book of magic which had never been translated, until Fox asked the snakes for help. The snakes writhed and curled on the ground, spelling out words, letter by letter, with their bodies. As they translated the book for Fox, they hissed and steamed. They became fiery lines on the ground, and then they burnt away entirely. Fox cried. That's the only time anyone has ever seen Fox cry, ever. She isn't like Prince Wing. Prince Wing is a crybaby.

The thing about *The Library* is that characters don't come back when they die. It's as if death is for real. So maybe Fox really is dead and she really isn't coming back. There are a couple of ghosts who hang around The Library looking for blood libations, but they've always been ghosts, all the way back to the beginning of the show. There aren't any evil twins or vampires, either. Although someday, hopefully, there will be evil twins. Who doesn't love evil twins?

"Mom told me about how you wrote about me," Jeremy says. His mother is still in the garage. He feels like a tennis ball in a game where the tennis players love him very, very much, even while they lob and smash and send him back and forth, back and forth.

His father says, "She said she wasn't going to tell you, but I guess I'm glad she did. I'm sorry, Germ. Are you hungry?"

"She's going out to Las Vegas next week. She wants me to go with her," Jeremy says.

"I know," his father says, still holding out a bowl of upside-down pizza. "Try not to worry about all of this, if you can. Think of it as an adventure."

"Mom says that's a stupid thing to say. Are you going to let me read the book with me in it?" Jeremy says.

"No," his father says, looking straight at Jeremy. "I burned it."

"Really?" Jeremy says. "Did you set fire to your computer, too?"

"Well, no," his father says. "But you can't read it. It wasn't any good, anyway. Come watch *The Library* with me. And will you eat some damn pizza, please? I may be a lousy father, but I'm a good cook. And if you love me, you'll eat the damn pizza and be grateful."

So they go sit on the orange couch and Jeremy eats pizza and watches *The Library* for the second-and-a-half time with his father. The lights on the timer in the living room go off, and Prince Wing kills Fox again. And then Jeremy goes to bed. His father goes away to write or to burn stuff. Whatever. His mother is still out in the garage.

On Jeremy's desk is a scrap of paper with a phone number on it. If he wanted to, he could call his phone booth. When he dials the number, it rings for a long time. Jeremy sits on his bed in the dark and listens to it ringing and ringing. When someone picks it up, he almost hangs up. Someone doesn't say anything, so Jeremy says, "Hello? Hello?"

Someone breathes into the phone on the other end of the line. Someone says in a soft, musical, squeaky voice, "Can't talk now, kid. Call back later." Then someone hangs up.

Jeremy dreams that he's sitting beside Fox on a sofa that his father has reupholstered in spider silk. His father has been stealing spiderwebs from the giant-spider superstores. From his own books. Is that shoplifting or is it self-plagiarism? The sofa is soft and gray and a little bit sticky. Fox sits on either side of him. The right-hand-side Fox is being played by Talis. Elizabeth plays the Fox on his left. Both Foxes look at him with enormous compassion.

"Are you dead?" Jeremy says.

"Are you?" the Fox who is being played by Elizabeth says, in that unmistakable Fox voice which, Jeremy's father once said, sounds like a sexy and demented helium balloon. It makes Jeremy's brain hurt, to hear Fox's voice coming out of Elizabeth's mouth.

The Fox who looks like Talis doesn't say anything at all. The writing on her T-shirt is so small and so foreign that Jeremy can't read it without feeling as if he's staring at Fox-Talis's breasts. It's probably something he needs to know, but he'll never be able to read it. He's too polite, and besides he's terrible at foreign languages.

"Hey, look," Jeremy says. "We're on TV!" There he is on television, sitting between two Foxes on a sticky gray couch in a field of red poppies. "Are we in Las Vegas?"

"We're not in Kansas," Fox-Elizabeth says. "There's something I need you to do for me."

"What's that?" Jeremy says.

"If I tell you in the dream," Fox-Elizabeth says, "you won't remember. You have to remember to call me when you're awake. Keep on calling until you get me."

"How will I remember to call you," Jeremy says, "if I don't remember what you tell me in this dream? Why do you need me to help you? Why is Talis here? What does her T-shirt say? Why are you both Fox? Is this Mars?"

Fox-Talis goes on watching TV. Fox-Elizabeth opens her kind and beautiful un-Hello-Kitty-like mouth again. She tells Jeremy the whole story. She explains everything. She translates Fox-Talis's T-shirt, which turns out to explain everything about Talis that Jeremy has ever wondered about. It answers every single question that Jeremy has ever had about girls. And then Jeremy wakes up—

It's dark. Jeremy flips on the light. The dream is moving away from him. There was something about Mars. Elizabeth was asking who he thought was prettier, Talis or Elizabeth. They were laughing. They both had pointy fox ears. They wanted him to do something. There was a telephone number he was supposed to call. There was something he was supposed to do.

In two weeks, on the fifteenth of April, Jeremy and his mother will get in her van and start driving out to Las Vegas. Every morning before school, Jeremy takes long showers and his father doesn't say anything at all. One day it's as if nothing is wrong between his parents. The next day they won't even look at each other. Jeremy's father won't come out of his study. And then the day after that, Jeremy comes home and finds his mother sitting on his father's lap. They're smiling as if they know something stupid and secret. They don't even notice Jeremy when he walks through the room. Even this is preferable, though, to the way they behave when they do notice him. They act guilty and strange and as if they are about to ruin his life. Gordon Mars makes pancakes every morning, and Jeremy's favorite dinner, macaroni and cheese, every night. Jeremy's mother plans out an itinerary for their trip. They will be stopping at libraries across the country, because his mother loves libraries. But she's also bought a new two-man tent and two sleeping bags and a portable stove, so that they can camp, if Jeremy wants to camp. Even though Jeremy's mother hates the outdoors.

Right after she does this, Gordon Mars spends all weekend in the garage. He won't let either of them see what he's doing, and when he does let them in, it turns out that he's removed the seating in the back of the van and bolted down two of his couches, one on each side, both upholstered in electric-blue fake fur.

They have to climb in through the cargo door at the back because one of the couches is blocking the sliding door. Jeremy's father says, looking very pleased with himself, "So now you don't have to camp outside, unless you want to. You can sleep inside. There's space underneath for suitcases. The sofas even have seat belts."

Over the sofas, Jeremy's father has rigged up small wooden shelves that fold down on chains from the walls of the van and become table tops. There's a travel-sized disco ball dangling from the ceiling, and a wooden panel—with Velcro straps and a black, quilted pad—behind the driver's seat, where Jeremy's father explains they can hang up the painting of the woman with the apple and the knife.

The van looks like something out of an episode of *The Library*. Jeremy's mother bursts into tears. She runs back inside the house. Jeremy's father says, helplessly, "I just wanted to make her laugh."

Jeremy wants to say, "I hate both of you." But he doesn't say it, and he doesn't. It would be easier if he did.

When Jeremy told Karl about Las Vegas, Karl punched him in the stomach. Then he said, "Have you told Talis?"

Jeremy said, "You're supposed to be nice to me! You're supposed to tell me not to go and that this sucks and you're not supposed to punch me. Why did you punch me? Is Talis all you ever think about?"

"Kind of," Karl said. "Most of the time. Sorry, Germ, of course I wish you weren't going and yeah, it also pisses me off. We're supposed to be best friends, but you do stuff all the time and I never get to. I've never driven across the country or been to Las Vegas, even though I'd really, really like to. I can't feel sorry for you when I bet you anything that while you're there, you'll sneak into some casino and play slot machines and win like a million bucks. You should feel sorry for me. I'm the one that has to stay here. Can I borrow your dirt bike while you're gone?"

"Sure," Jeremy said.

"How about your telescope?" Karl said.

"I'm taking it with me," Jeremy said.

"Fine. You have to call me every day," Karl said. "You have to e-mail. You have to tell me about Las Vegas show girls. I want to know how tall they really are. Whose phone number is this?"

Karl was holding the scrap of paper with the number of Jeremy's phone booth.

"Mine," Jeremy said. "That's my phone booth. The one I inherited."

"Have you called it?" Karl said.

"No," Jeremy said. He'd called the phone booth a few times. But it wasn't a game. Karl would think it was a game.

"Cool," Karl said and he went ahead and dialed the number. "Hello?" Karl said, "I'd like to speak to the person in charge of Jeremy's life. This is Jeremy's best friend, Karl."

"Not funny," Jeremy said.

"My life is boring," Karl said, into the phone. "I've never inherited anything. This girl I like won't talk to me. So is someone there? Does anybody want to talk to me? Does anyone want to talk to my friend, the Lord of the Phone Booth? Jeremy, they're demanding that you liberate the phone booth from yourself."

"Still not funny," Jeremy said and Karl hung up the phone.

This is how Jeremy told Elizabeth. They were up on the roof of Jeremy's house and he told her the whole thing. Not just the part about Las Vegas, but also the part about his father and how he put Jeremy in a book with no giant spiders in it.

"Have you read it?" Elizabeth said.

"No," Jeremy said. "He won't let me. Don't tell Karl. All I told him is that my mom and I have to go out for a few months to check out the wedding chapel."

"I won't tell Karl," Elizabeth said. She leaned forward and kissed Jeremy and then she wasn't kissing him. It was all very fast and surprising, but they didn't fall off the roof. Nobody falls off the roof in this story. "Talis likes you," Elizabeth said. "That's what Amy says. Maybe you like her back. I don't know. But I thought I should go ahead and kiss you now. Just in case I don't get to kiss you again."

"You can kiss me again," Jeremy said. "Talis probably doesn't like me."

"No," Elizabeth said. "I mean, let's not. I want to stay friends and it's hard enough to be friends, Germ. Look at you and Karl."

"I would never kiss Karl," Jeremy said.

"Funny, Germ. We should have a surprise party for you before you go," Elizabeth said.

"It won't be a surprise party now," Jeremy said. Maybe kissing him once was enough.

"Well, once I tell Amy it can't really be a surprise party,"

Elizabeth said. "She would explode into a million pieces and all the little pieces would start yelling, 'Guess what? Guess what? We're having a surprise party for you, Jeremy!' But just because I'm letting you in on the surprise doesn't mean there won't be surprises."

"I don't actually like surprises," Jeremy said.

"Who does?" Elizabeth said. "Only the people who do the surprising. Can we have the party at your house? I think it should be like Halloween, and it always feels like Halloween here. We could all show up in costumes and watch lots of old episodes of *The Library* and eat ice cream."

"Sure," Jeremy said. And then: "This is terrible! What if there's a new episode of *The Library* while I'm gone? Who am I going to watch it with?"

And he'd said the perfect thing. Elizabeth felt so bad about Jeremy having to watch *The Library* all by himself that she kissed him again.

There has never been a giant spider in any episode of *The Library*, although once Fox got really small and Ptolemy Krill carried her around in his pocket. She had to rip up one of Krill's handkerchiefs and blindfold herself, just in case she accidentally read a draft of Krill's terrible poetry. And then it turned out that, as well as the poetry, Krill's pocket also contained a rare, horned Anubis earwig that hadn't been properly preserved. Ptolemy Krill, it turned out, was careless with his kill jar. The earwig almost ate Fox, but instead it became her friend. It still sends her Christmas cards.

These are the two most important things that Jeremy and his friends have in common: a geographical location, and love of a television show about a library. Jeremy turns on the television as soon as he comes home from school. He flips through the channels, watching reruns of *Star Trek* and *Law & Order*. If there's a new episode of *The Library* before he and his mother leave for Las Vegas, then everything will be fine. Everything will work out. His mother says, "You watch too much television, Jeremy." But he goes on flipping through channels. Then he goes up to his room and makes phone calls.

"The new episode needs to be soon, because we're getting ready to leave. Tonight would be good. You'd tell me if there was going to be a new episode tonight, right?"

Silence.

"Can I take that as a yes? It would be easier if I had a brother," Jeremy tells his telephone booth. "Hello? Are you there? Or a sister. I'm tired of being good all the time. If I had a sibling, then we could take turns being good. If I had an older brother, I might be better at being bad, better at being angry. Karl is really good at being angry. He learned how from his brothers. I wouldn't want brothers like Karl's brothers, of course, but it sucks having to figure out everything all by myself. And the more normal I try to be, the more my parents think that I'm acting out. They think it's a phase that I'll grow out of. They think it isn't normal to be normal. Because there's no such thing as normal.

"And this whole book thing. The whole shoplifting thing, how my dad steals things, it figures that he went and stole my life. It isn't just me being melodramatic, to say that. That's exactly what he did! Did I tell you that once he stole a ferret from a pet store because he felt bad for it, and then he let it loose in our house and it turned out that it was pregnant? There was this woman who came to interview Dad and she sat down on one of the—"

Someone knocks on his bedroom door. "Jeremy?" his mother says.

Jeremy hangs up quickly. He's gotten into the habit of calling his phone booth every day. When he calls, it rings and rings and then it stops ringing, as if someone has picked up. There's just silence on the other end, no squeaky pretend-Fox voice, but it's a peaceful, interested silence. Jeremy complains about all the things there are to complain about, and the silent person on the other end listens and listens. Maybe it is Fox standing there in his phone booth and listening patiently. He wonders what incarnation of Fox is listening. One thing about Fox: she's never sorry for herself. She's always too busy. If it were really Fox, she'd hang up on him.

Jeremy opens his door. "I was on the phone," he says. His mother comes in and sits down on his bed. She's wearing one of his father's old flannel shirts. "All packed up?"

Jeremy shrugs. "I guess," he says. "Why did you cry when you saw what Dad did to the van? Don't you like it?"

"It's that painting," his mother says. "It was the first nice thing he ever gave me. We should have spent the money on health insurance. A new roof. Groceries! And instead he bought a painting. So I got angry. I left him. I took the painting and I moved into a hotel and I stayed there for three days. I was going to sell the painting, but then I decided I liked it instead. I came home."

She puts her hand on Jeremy's head, rubs it. "When I got pregnant with you I was hungry all the time but I couldn't eat. I'd have a dream that someone was going to give me a beautiful apple, like the one she's holding. When I told your father, he said he didn't trust her. He says she's holding out the apple like that as a trick and if you try to take it from her, she'll stab you with the peeling knife. He says that she's a tough old broad and she'll take care of us while we're on the road."

"Do we really have to go?" Jeremy says. "If we go to Las Vegas I might get into trouble. I might start using drugs or gambling or something."

"Oh, Germ. You try so hard to be a good kid," his mother says. "You try so hard to be normal. Sometimes I'd like to be normal, too. Maybe Vegas will be good for us. Are these the books that you're bringing?"

Jeremy shrugs. "I can't decide which ones I should take and which ones I can leave. It feels like whatever I leave behind, I'm leaving behind for good."

"That's silly," his mother says. "We're coming back. I promise. Your father and I will work things out. If you leave something behind that you need, he can mail it to you. Do you think there are slot machines in the libraries in Las Vegas? I talked to a woman at the Hell's Bells chapel and there's something called The Arts and Lovecraft Library where they keep Cleo's special collection of horror novels and gothic romances. You go in and out through a secret, swinging-bookcase door. People get married in it. There's a Dr. Frankenstein's LoveLab, The Masque of the Red Death Ballroom, and also something just called The Crypt. There's also The Vampire's Patio and The Black Lagoon Grotto, where you can get married by moonlight."

"You hate all this stuff," Jeremy says.

"It's not my cup of tea," his mother admits. Then she says, "When is everyone coming over?"

"Around eight," Jeremy says. "Are you going to get dressed up?"

"I don't have to dress up," his mother says. "I'm a librarian, remember?"

Jeremy's father's office is above the garage. In theory, no one is meant to interrupt him while he's working, but in practice Jeremy's father loves nothing better than to be interrupted, as long as the person who interrupts brings him something to eat. When Jeremy and his mother are gone, who will bring Jeremy's father food? Jeremy hardens his heart.

The floor is covered with books and bolts and samples of upholstering fabrics. Jeremy's father is lying facedown on the floor with his feet propped up on a bolt of fabric, which means that he is thinking and also that his back hurts. He claims to think best when he is on the verge of falling asleep.

"I brought you a bowl of Froot Loops," Jeremy says.

His father rolls over and looks up. "Thanks," he says. "What time is it? Is everyone here? Is that your costume? Is that my tuxedo jacket?"

"It's five-ish. Nobody's here yet. Do you like it?" Jeremy says. He's dressed as a Forbidden Book. His father's jacket is too big, but he still feels very elegant. Very sinister. His mother lent him the lipstick and the feathers and the platform heels.

"It's interesting," his father allows. "And a little frightening."

Jeremy feels obscurely pleased, even though he knows that his father is more amused than frightened. "Everyone else will probably come as Fox or Prince Wing. Except for Karl. He's coming as Ptolemy Krill. He even wrote some really bad poetry. I wanted to ask you something, before we leave tomorrow."

"Shoot," his father says.

"Did you really get rid of the novel with me in it?"

"No," his father says. "It felt unlucky. Unlucky to keep it, unlucky not to keep it. I don't know what to do with it."

Jeremy says, "I'm glad you didn't get rid of it."

"It's not any good, you know," his father says. "Which makes all this even worse. At first it was because I was bored with giant spiders. It was going to be something funny to show you. But then I wrote that you had a brain tumor and it wasn't funny any more. I figured I could save you—I'm the author, after all—but you got sicker and sicker. You were going through a rebellious phase. You were sneaking out of the house a lot and you hit your mother. You were a real jerk. But it turned out you had a brain tumor and it was making you behave strangely."

"Can I ask another question?" Jeremy says, deciding to take advantage while his father is still vulnerable.

"Go ahead," says his father.

"Could you not steal things for a while, if I asked you to?" Jeremy says. "Mom isn't going to be around to pay for the books and stuff that you steal. I don't want you to end up in jail because we went to Las Vegas."

His father closes his eyes as if he hopes Jeremy will forget that he asked a question, and go away.

Jeremy says nothing.

"All right," his father says finally. "I won't shoplift anything until you get home again."

Jeremy's mother runs around taking photos of everyone. Talis and Elizabeth have both shown up as Fox, although Talis is dead Fox. She carries her fake fur ears and tail around in a little see-through plastic purse and she also has a sword, which she leaves in the umbrella stand in the kitchen. Jeremy and Talis haven't talked much since she had a dream about him and since he told her that he's going to Las Vegas. She didn't say anything about that. Which is perfectly normal for Talis.

Karl makes an excellent Ptolemy Krill. Jeremy's Forbidden Book disguise is admired.

Amy's Faithful Margaret costume is almost as good as anything Faithful Margaret wears on TV. There are even special effects: Amy has rigged up her hair with red ribbons and wire and spray color and egg whites so that it looks as if it's on fire, and there are tiny papier-mâché golems in it, making horrible faces. She dances a polka with Jeremy's father. Faithful Margaret is mad for polka dancing.

No one has dressed up as Prince Wing.

They watch the episode with the possessed chicken and they watch the episode with the Salt Wife and they watch the episode where Prince Wing and Faithful Margaret fall under a spell and swap bodies and have sex for the first time. They watch the episode where Fox saves Prince Wing's life for the first time.

Jeremy's father makes chocolate/mango/espresso milk shakes for everyone. None of Jeremy's friends, except for Elizabeth, know about the novel. Everyone thinks Jeremy and his mother are just having an adventure. Everyone thinks Jeremy will be back at the end of the summer.

"I wonder how they find the actors," Elizabeth says. "They aren't real actors. They must be regular people. But you'd think that somewhere there would be someone who knows them. That somebody online would say, hey, that's my sister! Or that's the kid I went to school with who threw up in P.E. You know, sometimes someone says something like that or sometimes someone pretends that they know something about *The Library*, but it always turns out to be a hoax. Just somebody wanting to be somebody."

"What about the guy who's writing it?" Karl says.

Talis says, "Who says it's a guy?" and Amy says, "Yeah, Karl, why do you always assume it's a guy writing it?"

"Maybe nobody's writing it," Elizabeth says. "Maybe it's

magic or it's broadcast from outer space. Maybe it's real. Wouldn't that be cool?"

"No," Jeremy says. "Because then Fox would really be dead. That would suck."

"I don't care," Elizabeth says. "I wish it were real, anyway. Maybe it all really happened somewhere, like King Arthur or Robin Hood, and this is just one version of how it happened. Like a magical After School Special."

"Even if it isn't real," Amy says, "parts of it could be real. Like maybe the World-Tree Library is real. Or maybe *The Library* is made up, but Fox is based on somebody that the writer knew. Writers do that all the time, right? Jeremy, I think your dad should write a book about me. I could be eaten by giant spiders. Or have sex with giant spiders and have spider babies. I think that would be so great."

So Amy does have psychic abilities, after all, although hopefully she will never know this. When Jeremy tests his own potential psychic abilities, he can almost sense his father, hovering somewhere just outside the living room, listening to this conversation and maybe even taking notes. Which is what writers do. But Jeremy isn't really psychic. It's just that lurking and hovering and appearing suddenly when you weren't expecting him are what his father does, just like shoplifting and cooking. Jeremy prays to all the dark gods that he never receives the gift of knowing what people are thinking. It's a dark road and it ends up with you trapped on late-night television in front of an invisible audience of depressed insomniacs wearing hats made out of tinfoil, and they all want to pay you nine-ninety-nine per minute to hear you describe in minute, terrible detail what their deceased cat is thinking about, right now. What kind of future is that? He wants to go to Mars. And when will Elizabeth kiss him again?

You can't just kiss someone twice and then never kiss them again. He tries not to think about Elizabeth and kissing, just in case Amy reads his mind. He realizes that he's been staring at Talis's breasts, glares instead at Elizabeth, who is watching TV. Meanwhile, Karl is glaring at him.

On television, Fox is dancing in the Invisible Nightclub with Faithful Margaret, whose hair is about to catch fire again. The Norns are playing their screechy cover of "Come On Eileen." The Norns only know two songs: "Come On Eileen" and "Everybody Wants to Rule the World." They don't play real instruments. They play squeaky dog toys and also a bathtub, which is enchanted, although nobody knows who by, or why or what it was enchanted for.

"If you had to choose one," Jeremy says, "invisibility or the ability to fly, which would you choose?"

Everybody looks at him. "Only perverts want to be invisible," Elizabeth says. "So they can spy on people. Or rob banks. You can't trust invisible people."

"You'd have to be naked if you were invisible," Karl says. "Because otherwise people would see your clothes."

"If you could fly, you'd have to wear thermal underwear because it's cold up there. So it just depends on whether you like to wear long underwear or no underwear at all," Amy says.

It's the kind of conversation that they have all the time. It makes Jeremy feel homesick even though he hasn't left yet.

"Maybe I'll go make brownies," Jeremy says. "Elizabeth, do you want to help me make brownies?"

"Shhh," Elizabeth says. "This is a good part."

On television, Fox and Faithful Margaret are making out. The Faithful part is kind of a joke.

Jeremy's parents go to bed at some point. By three, Amy and Elizabeth are passed out on the couch and Karl has gone upstairs to check his e-mail on Jeremy's iBook. On TV, wolves are roaming the tundra of The Free People's World-Tree Library's fortieth floor. Snow is falling heavily and librarians are burning books to keep warm, but only the most dull and improving works of literature.

Jeremy isn't sure where Talis has gone, so he goes to look for her. She hasn't gone far. She's on the landing, looking at the space on the wall where Alice Mars's painting should be hanging. Talis is carrying her sword with her, and her little plastic purse. In the bathroom off the landing, the singing toilet is still singing away.

"We're taking the painting with us," Jeremy says. "My dad insisted, just in case he accidentally burns down the house while we're gone. Do you want to go see it? I was going to show everybody, but everybody's asleep right now."

"Sure," Talis says.

So Jeremy gets a flashlight and takes her out to the garage and shows her the van. She climbs right inside and sits down on one of the blue-fur couches. She looks around and he wonders what she's thinking. He wonders if the toilet song is stuck in her head.

"My dad did all of this," Jeremy says. He turns on the flashlight and shines it on the disco ball. Light spatters off in anxious, slippery orbits. Jeremy shows Talis how his father has hung up the painting. It looks truly wrong in the van, as if someone demented put it there. Especially with the light reflecting off the disco ball. The woman in the painting looks confused and embarrassed, as if Jeremy's father has accidentally canceled out her protective powers. Maybe the disco ball is her Kryptonite.

"So remember how you had a dream about me?" Jeremy says. Talis nods. "I think I had a dream about you, that you were Fox."

Talis opens up her arms, encompassing her costume, her sword, her plastic purse with poor Fox's ears and tail inside.

"There was something you wanted me to do," Jeremy says. "I was supposed to save you, somehow."

Talis just looks at him.

"How come you never talk?" Jeremy says. All of this is irritating. How he used to feel normal around Elizabeth, like friends, and now everything is peculiar and uncomfortable. How he used to enjoy feeling uncomfortable around Talis, and now, suddenly, he doesn't. This must be what sex is about. Stop thinking about sex, he thinks.

Talis opens her mouth and closes it again. Then she says, "I don't know. Amy talks so much. You all talk a lot. Somebody has to be the person who doesn't. The person who listens."

"Oh," Jeremy says. "I thought maybe you had a tragic secret. Like maybe you used to stutter." Except secrets can't have secrets, they just *are*.

"Nope," Talis says. "It's like being invisible, you know. Not talking. I like it."

"But you're not invisible," Jeremy says. "Not to me. Not to Karl. Karl really likes you. Did you hit him with a boa constrictor on purpose?"

But Talis says, "I wish you weren't leaving." The disco ball spins and spins. It makes Jeremy feel kind of carsick and also, looking down at his arms, as if he has sparkly, disco leprosy. He doesn't say anything back to Talis, just to see how it feels. Except maybe that's rude. Or maybe it's rude the way everybody always talks and doesn't leave any space for Talis to say anything.

"At least you get to miss school," Talis says, at last.

"Yeah," he says. He leaves another space, but Talis doesn't say anything this time. "We're going to stop at all these museums and things on the way across the country. I'm supposed to keep a blog for school and describe stuff in it. I'm going to make a lot of stuff up. So it will be like Creative Writing and not so much like homework."

"You should make a list of all the towns with weird names you drive through," Talis says. "Town of Horseheads. That's a real place."

"Plantagenet," Jeremy says. "That's a real place, too. I had something really weird to tell you."

Talis waits, like she always does.

Jeremy says, "I called my phone booth, the one that I inherited, and someone answered. She sounded just like Fox and she told me—she told me to call back later. So I've called a few more times, but I don't ever get her."

"Fox isn't a real person," Talis says. "*The Library* is just TV." But she sounds uncertain. That's the thing about *The Library*. Nobody knows for sure. Everyone who watches it wishes and hopes that it's not just acting. That it's magic. Real magic.

"I know," Jeremy says.

"I wish Fox was real," Fox-Talis says.

They've been sitting in the van for a long time. If Karl looks for them and can't find them, he's going to think that they've been making out. He'll kill Jeremy. Once Karl tried to strangle another kid for accidentally peeing on his shoes. Jeremy might as well kiss Talis. So he does, even though she's still holding her sword. She doesn't hit him with it. It's dark and he has his eyes closed and he can almost imagine that he's kissing Elizabeth.

Karl has fallen asleep on Jeremy's bed. Talis is downstairs, fast-forwarding through the episode where some librarians drink too much Euphoria and decide to abolish Story Hour. Not just the practice of having a Story Hour, but the whole Hour. Amy and Elizabeth are still sacked out on the couch. It's weird to watch Amy sleep. She doesn't talk in her sleep.

Karl is snoring. Jeremy could go up on the roof and look at stars, except he's already packed up his telescope. He could try to wake up Elizabeth and they could go up on the roof, but Talis is down there. He and Talis could go sit on the roof, but he doesn't want to kiss Talis on the roof. He makes a solemn oath to only ever kiss Elizabeth on the roof.

He picks up his phone. Maybe he can call his phone booth and complain just a little and not wake Karl up. His dad is going to freak out about the phone bill. All these calls to Nevada. It's 4 A.M. Jeremy's plan is not to go to sleep at all. His friends are lame.

The phone rings and rings and rings and then someone picks up. Jeremy recognizes the silence on the other end. "Everybody came over and fell asleep," he whispers. "That's why I'm whispering. I don't even think they care that I'm leaving. And my feet hurt. Remember how I was going to dress up as a Forbidden Book? Platform shoes aren't comfortable. Karl thinks I did it on purpose, to be even taller than him than usual. And I forgot that I was wearing lipstick and I kissed Talis and got lipstick all over her face, so it's a good thing everyone was asleep because otherwise someone would have seen. And my dad says that he won't shoplift at all while Mom and I are gone, but you can't trust him. And that fake-fur upholstery sheds like—"

"Jeremy," that strangely familiar, sweet-and-rusty door-hinge voice says softly. "Shut up, Jeremy. I need your help."

"Wow!" Jeremy says, not in a whisper. "Wow, wow, wow! Is this Fox? Are you really Fox? Is this a joke? Are you real? Are you dead? What are you doing in my phone booth?"

"You know who I am," Fox says, and Jeremy knows with all his heart that it's really Fox. "I need you to do something for me."

"What?" Jeremy says. Karl, on the bed, laughs in his sleep as if the idea of Jeremy doing something is funny to him. "What could I do?"

"I need you to steal three books," Fox says. "From a library in a place called Iowa."

"I know Iowa," Jeremy says. "I mean, I've never been there, but it's a real place. I could go there."

"I'm going to tell you the books you need to steal," Fox says. "Author, title, and the jewelly festival number—"

"Dewey decimal," Jeremy says. "It's actually called the Dewey decimal number in real libraries."

"Real," Fox says, sounding amused. "You need to write this all down and also how to get to the library. You need to steal the three books and bring them to me. It's very important."

"Is it dangerous?" Jeremy says. "Are the Forbidden Books up to something? Are the Forbidden Books real, too? What if I get caught stealing?"

"It's not dangerous to you," Fox says. "Just don't get caught. Remember the episode of *The Library* when I was the old woman with the beehive and I stole the Bishop of Tweedle's false teeth while he was reading the banns for the wedding of Faithful Margaret and Sir Petronella the Younger? Remember how he didn't even notice?"

"I've never seen that episode," Jeremy says, although as far as he knows he's never missed a single episode of *The Library*. He's never even heard of Sir Petronella.

"Oh," Fox says. "Maybe that's a flashback in a later episode or something. That's a great episode. We're depending on you, Jeremy. You have got to steal these books. They contain dreadful secrets. I can't say the titles out loud. I'm going to spell them instead."

So Jeremy gets a pad of paper and Fox spells out the titles of each book twice. (They aren't titles that can be written down here. It's safer not to even think about some books.) "Can I ask you something?" Jeremy says. "Can I tell anybody about this? Not Amy. But could I tell Karl or Elizabeth? Or Talis? Can I tell my mom? If I woke up Karl right now, would you talk to him for a minute?"

"I don't have a lot of time," Fox says. "I have to go now. Please don't tell anyone, Jeremy. I'm sorry."

"Is it the Forbidden Books?" Jeremy says again. What would Fox think if she saw the costume he's still wearing, all except for the platform heels? "Do you think I shouldn't trust my friends? But I've known them my whole life!"

Fox makes a noise, a kind of pained whuff.

"What is it?" Jeremy says. "Are you okay?"

"I have to go," Fox says. "Nobody can know about this. Don't give anybody this number. Don't tell anyone about your phone booth. Or me. Promise, Germ?"

"Only if you promise you won't call me Germ," Jeremy says, feeling really stupid. "I hate when people call me that. Call me Mars instead."

"Mars," Fox says, and it sounds exotic and strange and brave, as if Jeremy has just become a new person, a person named after a whole planet, a person who kisses girls and talks to Foxes.

"I've never stolen anything," Jeremy says.

But Fox has hung up.

Maybe out there, somewhere, is someone who enjoys having to say good-bye, but it isn't anyone that Jeremy knows. All of his friends are grumpy and red-eyed, although not from crying. From lack of sleep. From too much television. There are still faint red stains around Talis's mouth, and if everyone wasn't so tired, they would realize it's Jeremy's lipstick. Karl gives Jeremy a handful of quarters, dimes, nickels, and pennies. "For the slot machines," Karl says. "If you win anything, you can keep a third of what you win."

"Half," Jeremy says, automatically.

"Fine," Karl says. "It's all from your dad's sofas, anyway. Just one more thing. Stop getting taller. Don't get taller while you're gone. Okay." He hugs Jeremy hard: so hard that it's almost like getting punched again. No wonder Talis threw the boa constrictor at Karl.

Talis and Elizabeth both hug Jeremy good-bye. Talis looks even more mysterious now that he's sat with her under a disco ball and made out. Later on, Jeremy will discover that Talis has left her sword under the blue-fur couch and he'll wonder if she left it on purpose.

Talis doesn't say anything and Amy, of course, doesn't shut up, not even when she kisses him. It feels weird to be kissed by someone who goes right on talking while they kiss you, and yet it shouldn't be a surprise that Amy kisses him. He imagines that later Amy and Talis and Elizabeth will all compare notes.

Elizabeth says, "So I promise to tape every episode of *The Library* while you're gone so we can all watch them together when you get back. And I promise I'll call you in Vegas, no matter what time it is there, when there's a new episode."

Her hair is a mess and her breath is faintly sour. Jeremy

wishes he could tell her how beautiful she looks. "I'll write bad poetry and send it to you," he says.

Jeremy's mother is looking hideously cheerful as she goes in and out of the house, making sure that she hasn't left anything behind. She loves long car trips. It doesn't seem to bother her one bit that she and her son are abandoning their entire lives. She passes Jeremy a folder full of maps. "You're in charge of not getting lost," she says. "Put these somewhere safe."

Jeremy says, "I found a library online that I want to go visit. Out in Iowa. They have a corn mosaic on the façade of the building, with a lot of naked goddesses and gods dancing around in a field of corn. Someone wants to take it down. Can we go see it first?"

His mother gives him a pleased, conspiratorial look. "Of course," she says.

Jeremy's father has filled a whole grocery bag with sandwiches. His hair is drooping and he looks even more like an ax murderer than usual. If this were a movie, you'd think that Jeremy and his mother were escaping in the nick of time. "You take care of your mother," he says to Jeremy.

"Sure," Jeremy says. "You take care of yourself."

His dad sags. "You take care of yourself, too." So it's settled. They're all supposed to take care of themselves. Why can't they stay home and take care of each other, until Jeremy is good and ready to go off to college? "I've got another bag of sandwiches in the kitchen," his dad says. "I should go get them."

"Wait," Jeremy says. "I have to ask you something before we take off. Suppose I had to steal something. I mean, I don't have to steal anything, of course, and I know stealing is wrong, even when *you* do it, and I would never steal anything. But what if I did? How do you do it? How do you do it and not get caught?"

His father shrugs. He's probably wondering if Jeremy is really his son. Gordon Mars inherited his mutant, long-fingered, ambidextrous hands from a long line of shoplifters and money launderers and petty criminals. They're all deeply ashamed of Jeremy's father. Gordon Mars had a gift and he threw it away to become a writer. "I don't know," he says. He picks up Jeremy's hand and looks at it as if he's never noticed before that Jeremy had something hanging off the end of his wrist. "You just do it. You do it like you're not really doing anything at all. You do it while you're thinking about something else and you forget that you're doing it."

Jeremy takes his hand back. "I'm not planning on stealing anything. I was just curious."

His father looks at him. "Take care of yourself," he says again, as if he really means it, and hugs Jeremy hard.

Then he goes and gets the sandwiches (so many sandwiches that Jeremy and his mother will eat nothing but sandwiches for the first three days, and still have to throw half of them away). Everyone waves. Jeremy and his mother climb in the van. Jeremy's mother turns on the CD player. Bob Dylan is singing about monkeys. His mother loves Bob Dylan. They drive away.

Do you know how, sometimes, during a commercial break in your favorite television shows, your best friend calls and wants to talk about one of her boyfriends, and when you try to hang up, she starts crying and you try to cheer her up and end up missing about half of the episode? And so when you go to work, or to school the next day, you have to get the guy who sits next to you to explain what happened? That's the good thing about a book. You can mark your place in a book. But this isn't really a book. It's an episode of a television show called *The Library*.

In one episode of *The Library*, an adolescent boy drives across the country with his mother. They have to change a tire. The boy practices taking things out of his mother's purse and putting them back again. He steals a sixteen-ounce bottle of Coke from one convenience market and leaves it at another convenience market. The boy and his mother stop at a lot of libraries, and the boy keeps a blog, but he skips the bit about the library in Iowa. He writes in his blog about what he's reading, but he doesn't read the books he stole in Iowa, because Fox told him not to, and because he has to hide them from his mother. Well, he reads just a few pages. Skims, really. He hides them under the blue-fur sofa. They go camping in Utah, and the boy sets up his telescope. He sees three shooting stars and a coyote. He never sees anyone who looks like a Forbidden Book, although he sees a transvestite go into the women's restroom at a rest stop in Indiana. He calls a phone booth just outside Las Vegas twice, but no one ever answers. He has short conversations with his father. He wonders what his father is up to. He wishes he could tell his father about Fox and the books. Once the boy's mother finds a giant spider the size of an Oreo in their tent. She starts laughing hysterically. She takes a picture of it with her digital camera, and the boy puts the picture on his blog. Sometimes the boy asks questions and his mother talks about her parents. Once she cries. The boy doesn't know what to say. They talk about their favorite episodes of *The Library* and the episodes that they really hated, and the mother asks if the boy thinks Fox is really dead. He says he doesn't think so.

Once a man tries to break into the van while they are sleeping in it. But then he goes away. Maybe the painting of the woman with the peeling knife is protecting them.

But you've seen this episode before.

It's Cinco de Mayo. It's almost seven o'clock at night, and the sun is beginning to go down. Jeremy and his mother are in the desert and Las Vegas is somewhere in front of them. Every time they pass a driver coming the other way, Jeremy tries to figure out if that person has just won or lost a lot of money. Everything is flat and sort of tilted here, except off in the distance, where the land goes up abruptly, as if someone started to fold up a map. Somewhere around here is the Grand Canyon, which must have been a surprise when people first saw it.

Jeremy's mother says, "Are you sure we have to do this first? Couldn't we go find your phone booth later?"

"Can we do it now?" Jeremy says. "I said I was going to do it on my blog. It's like a quest that I have to complete."

"Okay," his mother says. "It should be around here somewhere. It's supposed to be four and a half miles after the turn-off, and here's the turn-off."

It isn't hard to find the phone booth. There isn't much else around. Jeremy should feel excited when he sees it, but it's a disappointment, really. He's seen phone booths before. He was expecting something to be different. Mostly he feels tired of road trips and tired of roads and just tired, tired, tired. He looks around to see if Fox is somewhere nearby, but there's just a hiker off in the distance.

"Okay, Germ," his mother says. "Make this quick."

"I need to get my backpack out of the back," Jeremy says.

"Do you want me to come, too?" his mother says.

"No," Jeremy says. "This is kind of personal."

His mother looks like she's trying not to laugh. "Just hurry up. I have to pee."

When Jeremy gets to the phone booth, he turns around. His

mother has the light on in the van. It looks like she's singing along to the radio. His mother has a terrible voice.

When he steps inside the phone booth, it isn't magical. The phone booth smells rank, as if an animal has been living in it. The windows are smudgy. He takes the stolen books out of his backpack and puts them in the little shelf where someone has stolen a phone book. Then he waits. Maybe Fox is going to call him. Maybe he's supposed to wait until she calls. But she doesn't call. He feels lonely. There's no one he can tell about this. He feels like an idiot and he also feels kind of proud. Because he did it. He drove cross-country with his mother and saved an imaginary person.

"So how's your phone booth?" his mother says.

"Great!" he says, and they're both silent again. Las Vegas is in front of them and then all around them and everything is lit up like they're inside a pinball game. All of the trees look fake. Like someone read too much Dr. Seuss and got ideas. People are walking up and down the sidewalks. Some of them look normal. Others look like they just escaped from a fancy-dress ball at a lunatic asylum. Jeremy hopes they've just won lots of money and that's why they look so startled, so strange. Or maybe they're all vampires.

"Left," he tells his mother. "Go left here. Look out for the vampires on the crosswalk. And then it's an immediate right." Four times his mother let him drive the van: once in Utah, twice in South Dakota, once in Pennsylvania. The van smells like old burger wrappers and fake fur, and it doesn't help that Jeremy's gotten used to the smell. The woman in the painting has had a pained expression on her face for the last few nights, and the disco ball has lost some of its pieces of mirror because Jeremy kept knocking his head on it in the morning. Jeremy and his mother haven't showered in three days.

Here is the wedding chapel, in front of them, at the end of a long driveway. Electric purple light shines on a sign that spells out HELL'S BELLS. There's a wrought-iron fence and a yard full of trees dripping Spanish moss. Under the trees, tombstones and miniature mausoleums.

"Do you think those are real?" his mother says. She sounds slightly worried.

"'Harry East, Recently Deceased,'" Jeremy says. "No, I don't."

There's a white hearse in the driveway with a little plaque on the back. *Recently ~~Buried~~ Married.* The chapel is a Victorian house with a bell tower. Perhaps it's full of bats. Or giant spiders. Jeremy's father would love this place. His mother is going to hate it.

Someone stands at the threshold of the chapel, door open, looking out at them. But as Jeremy and his mother get out of the van, he turns and goes inside and shuts the door. His mother says, "They've probably gone to put the boiling oil in the microwave."

She rings the doorbell determinedly. Instead of ringing, there's a recording of a crow. *Caw, caw, caw.* All the lights in the Victorian house go out. Then they turn on again. The door swings open and Jeremy tightens his grip on his backpack, just in case. "Good evening, Madam. Young man," a man says and Jeremy looks up and up and up. The man at the door has to lower his head to look out. His hands are large as toaster ovens. He looks like he's wearing Chihuahua coffins on his feet. Two realistic-looking bolts stick out on either side of his head. He wears green pancake makeup and glittery green eye shadow, and his lashes are as long and thick and green as AstroTurf. "We weren't expecting you so soon."

"We should have called ahead," Jeremy's mother says. "I'm so sorry."

"Great costume," Jeremy says.

The Frankenstein curls his lip in a somber way. "Thank you," he says. "Call me Miss Thing, please."

"I'm Jeremy," Jeremy says. "This is my mother."

"Oh please," Miss Thing says. Even his wink is somehow lugubrious. "You tease me. She isn't old enough to be your mother."

"Oh please, yourself," Jeremy's mother says.

"Quick, the two of you," someone yells from somewhere inside Hell's Bells. "While you zthtand there gabbing, the devil ithz prowling around like a lion, looking for a way to get in. Are you juthzt going to zthtand there and hold the door wide open for him?"

So they all step inside. "Iz that Jeremy Marthz at lathzt?" the voice says. "Earth to Marthz, Earth to Marthz. Marthzzz, Jeremy Marthzzz, there'thz zthomeone on the phone for Jeremy Marthz. She'thz called three timethz in the lathzt ten minutethz, Jeremy Marthzzzz."

It's Fox, Jeremy knows. Of course, it's Fox! She's in the phone booth. She's got the books and she's going to tell me that I saved whatever it is that I was saving. He walks toward the buzzing voice while Miss Thing and his mother go back out to the van.

He hurries past a room full of artfully draped spider webs and candelabras drooping with drippy candles. Someone is playing the organ behind a wooden screen. He goes down the hall and up a long staircase. The banisters are carved with little faces. Owls and foxes and ugly children. The voice goes on talking. "Yoohoo, Jeremy, up the stairthz, that'thz right. Now, come along, come right in! Not in there, in here, in here! Don't mind the dark, we *like* the dark, juthzt watch your zthep." Jeremy puts his hand out. He touches something and there's a click and the bookcase in front of him slowly slides back. Now the room is three times as large and there are more bookshelves and there's a young woman wearing dark sunglasses, sitting on a couch. She has a megaphone in one hand and a phone in the other. "For you, Jeremy Marth," she says. She's the palest person Jeremy has ever seen and her two canine teeth are so pointed that she lisps a little when she talks. On the megaphone the lisp was sinister, but now it just makes her sound irritable.

She hands him the phone. "Hello?" he says. He keeps an eye on the vampire.

"Jeremy!" Elizabeth says. "It's on, it's on, it's on! It's just started! We're all just sitting here. Everybody's here. What happened to your cell phone? We kept calling."

"Mom left it at the visitor's center in Zion," Jeremy says.

"Well, you're there. We figured out from your blog that you must be near Vegas. Amy says she had a feeling that you were going to get there in time. She made us keep calling. Stay on the phone, Jeremy. We can all watch it together, okay? Hold on."

Karl grabs the phone. "Hey, Germ, I didn't get any postcards," he says. "You forget how to write or something? Wait a minute. Somebody wants to say something to you." Then he laughs and laughs and passes the phone on to someone else who doesn't say anything at all.

"Talis?" Jeremy says.

Maybe it isn't Talis. Maybe it's Elizabeth again. He thinks about how his mouth is right next to Elizabeth's ear. Or maybe it's Talis's ear.

The vampire on the couch is already flipping through the channels. Jeremy would like to grab the remote away from her, but it's not a good idea to try to take things away from a vampire. His mother and Miss Thing come up the stairs and into the room and suddenly the room seems absolutely full of people, as if Karl and Amy and Elizabeth and Talis have come into the room, too. His hand is getting sweaty around the phone. Miss Thing has a firm hold on Jeremy's mother's painting, as if it might try to escape. Jeremy's mother looks tired. For the past three days her hair has been braided into pigtails. She looks younger to Jeremy, as if they've been traveling backward in time instead of just across the country. She smiles at Jeremy, a giddy, exhausted smile. Jeremy smiles back.

"Is it *The Library*?" Miss Thing says. "Is a new episode on?"

Jeremy sits down on the couch beside the vampire, still holding the phone to his ear. His arm is getting tired.

"I'm here," he says to Talis or Elizabeth or whoever it is on the other end of the phone. "I'm here." And then he sits and doesn't say anything and waits with everyone else for the vampire to find the right channel so they can all find out if he's saved Fox, if Fox is alive, if Fox is still alive.

Faeries live inside it.
I know what that sounds like, but it's true.

THE FAERY HANDBAG

I USED TO go to thrift stores with my friends. We'd take the train into Boston, and go to The Garment District, which is this huge vintage clothing warehouse. Everything is arranged by color, and somehow that makes all of the clothes beautiful. It's kind of like if you went through the wardrobe in the Narnia books, only instead of finding Aslan and the White Witch and horrible Eustace, you found this magic clothing world—instead of talking animals, there were feather boas and wedding dresses and bowling shoes, and paisley shirts and Doc Martens and everything hung up on racks so that first you have black dresses, all together, like the world's largest indoor funeral, and then blue dresses—all the blues you can imagine—and then red dresses and so on. Pink-reds and orangey-reds and purple-reds and exit-light reds and candy reds. Sometimes I'd close my eyes and Natasha and Natalie and Jake would drag me over to a rack, and rub a dress against my hand. "Guess what color this is."

We had this theory that you could learn how to tell, just by feeling, what color something was. For example, if you're sitting on a lawn, you can tell what color green the grass is with your eyes closed, depending on how silky rubbery it feels. With clothing, stretchy velvet stuff always feels red when your eyes are closed, even if it's not red. Natasha was always best at guessing colors, but Natasha is also best at cheating at games and not getting caught.

One time we were looking through kid's T-shirts and we found a Muppets T-shirt that had belonged to Natalie in third grade. We knew it belonged to her, because it still had her name inside, where her mother had written it in permanent marker when Natalie went to summer camp. Jake bought it back for her, because he was the only one who had money that weekend. He was the only one who had a job.

Maybe you're wondering what a guy like Jake is doing in The Garment District with a bunch of girls. The thing about Jake is that he always has a good time, no matter what he's doing. He likes everything, and he likes everyone, but he likes me best of all. Wherever he is now, I bet he's having a great time and wondering when I'm going to show up. I'm always running late. But he knows that.

We had this theory that things have life cycles, the way that people do. The life cycle of wedding dresses and feather boas and T-shirts and shoes and handbags involves The Garment District. If clothes are good, or even if they're bad in an interesting way, The Garment District is where they go when they die. You can tell that they're dead, because of the way that they smell. When you buy them, and wash them, and start wearing them again, and they start to smell like you, that's when they reincarnate. But the point is, if you're looking for a particular thing, you just have to keep looking for it. You have to look hard.

Down in the basement at The Garment District they sell clothing and beat-up suitcases and teacups by the pound. You can get eight pounds worth of prom dresses—a slinky black dress, a poufy lavender dress, a swirly pink dress, a silvery, starry lamé dress so fine you could pass it through a key ring—for eight dollars. I go there every week, hunting for Grandmother Zofia's faery handbag.

The faery handbag: It's huge and black and kind of hairy. Even when your eyes are closed, it feels black. As black as black ever gets, like if you touch it, your hand might get stuck in it, like tar or black quicksand or when you stretch out your hand at night, to turn on a light, but all you feel is darkness.

Faeries live inside it. I know what that sounds like, but it's true.

Grandmother Zofia said it was a family heirloom. She said that it was over two hundred years old. She said that when she died, I had to look after it. Be its guardian. She said that it would be my responsibility.

I said it didn't look that old, and that they didn't have handbags two hundred years ago, but that just made her cross. She said, "So then tell me, Genevieve, darling, where do you think old ladies used to put their reading glasses and their heart medicine and their knitting needles?"

I know no one is going to believe any of this. That's okay. If I thought you would, then I couldn't tell you. Promise me you won't believe a word. That's what Zofia used to say to me when she told me stories. At the funeral, my mother said, half laughing and half crying, that her mother was the world's best liar. I think she thought maybe Zofia wasn't really dead. But I went up to Zofia's coffin, and I looked her right in the eyes. They were closed. The funeral parlor had made her up with blue eye shadow and blue eyeliner. She looked like she was going to be a news anchor on Fox television, instead of dead. It was creepy and it made me even sadder than I already was. But I didn't let that distract me.

"Okay, Zofia," I whispered. "I know you're dead, but this is important. You know exactly how important this is. Where's the handbag? What did you do with it? How do I find it? What am I supposed to do now?"

Of course she didn't say a word. She just lay there, this little smile on her face, as if she thought the whole thing—death, blue eye shadow, Jake, the handbag, fairies, Scrabble, Baldeziwurlekistan, all of it—was a joke. She always did have a weird sense of humor. That's why she and Jake got along so well.

I grew up in a house next door to the house where my mother lived when she was a little girl. Her mother, Zofia Swink, my grandmother, babysat me while my mother and father were at work.

Zofia never looked like a grandmother. She had long black hair which she wore in little braided spiky towers and plaits. She had large blue eyes. She was taller than my father. She looked like a spy or ballerina or a lady pirate or a rock star. She acted like one, too. For example, she never drove anywhere. She rode a bike. It drove my mother crazy. "Why can't you act your age?" she'd say, and Zofia would just laugh.

Zofia and I played Scrabble all the time. Zofia always won, even though her English wasn't all that great, because we'd decided that she was allowed to use Baldeziwurleki vocabulary. Baldeziwurlekistan is where Zofia was born, over two hundred years ago. That's what Zofia said. (My grandmother claimed to be over two hundred years old. Or maybe even older. Sometimes she claimed that she'd even met Genghis Khan. He was much shorter than her. I probably don't have time to tell that story.) Baldeziwurlekistan is also an incredibly valuable word in Scrabble points, even though it doesn't exactly fit on the board. Zofia put it down the first time we played. I was feeling pretty good because I'd gotten forty-one points for "zippery" on my turn.

Zofia kept rearranging her letters on her tray. Then she looked over at me, as if daring me to stop her, and put down "eziwurlekistan," after "bald." She used "delicious," "zippery," "wishes," "kismet," and "needle," and made "to" into "toe." "Baldeziwurlekistan" went all the way across the board and then trailed off down the right-hand side.

I started laughing.

"I used up all my letters," Zofia said. She licked her pencil and started adding up points.

"That's not a word," I said. "Baldeziwurlekistan is not a word. Besides, you can't do that. You can't put an eighteen-letter word on a board that's fifteen squares across."

"Why not? It's a country," Zofia said. "It's where I was born, little darling."

"Challenge," I said. I went and got the dictionary and looked it up. "There's no such place."

"Of course there isn't nowadays," Zofia said. "It wasn't a very big place, even when it was a place. But you've heard of Samarkand, and Uzbekistan and the Silk Road and Genghis Khan. Haven't I told you about meeting Genghis Khan?"

I looked up Samarkand. "Okay," I said. "Samarkand is a real place. A real word. But Baldeziwurlekistan isn't."

"They call it something else now," Zofia said. "But I think it's important to remember where we come from. I think it's only fair that I get to use Baldeziwurleki words. Your English is so much better than me. Promise me something, mouthful of dumpling, a small, small thing. You'll remember its real name. Baldeziwurlekistan. Now when I add it up, I get three hundred and sixty-eight points. Could that be right?"

If you called the faery handbag by its right name, it would be something like "orzipanikanikcz," which means the "bag of skin where the world lives," only Zofia never spelled that word the same way twice. She said you had to spell it a little differently each time. You never wanted to spell it exactly the right way, because that would be dangerous.

I called it the faery handbag because I put "faery" down on the Scrabble board once. Zofia said that you spelled it with an *i* not an *e*. She looked it up in the dictionary, and lost a turn.

Zofia said that in Baldeziwurlekistan they used a board and tiles for divination, prognostication, and sometimes even just for fun. She said it was a little like playing Scrabble. That's probably why she turned out to be so good at Scrabble. The Baldeziwurlekistanians used their tiles and board to communicate with the people who lived under the hill. The people who lived under the hill knew the future. The Baldeziwurlekistanians gave them fermented milk and honey, and the young women of the village used to go and lie out on the hill and sleep under the stars. Apparently the people under the hill were pretty cute. The important thing was that you never went down into the hill and spent the night there, no matter how cute the guy from under the hill was. If you did, even if you only spent a single night under the hill, when you came out again a hundred years might have passed. "Remember that," Zofia said to me. "It doesn't matter how cute a guy is. If he wants you to come back to his place, it isn't a good idea. It's okay to fool around, but don't spend the night."

Every once in a while, a woman from under the hill would marry a man from the village, even though it never ended well. The problem was that the women under the hill were terrible cooks. They couldn't get used to the way time worked in the village, which meant that supper always got burnt, or else it wasn't cooked long enough. But they couldn't stand to be criticized. It hurt their feelings. If their village husband complained, or even if he looked like he wanted to complain, that was it. The woman from under the hill went back to her home, and even if her husband went and begged and pleaded and apologized, it might be three years or thirty years or a few generations before she came back out.

Even the best, happiest marriages between the Baldeziwurle-kistanians and the people under the hill fell apart when the children got old enough to complain about dinner. But everyone in the village had some hill blood in them.

"It's in you," Zofia said, and kissed me on the nose. "Passed down from my grandmother and her mother. It's why we're so beautiful."

When Zofia was nineteen, the shaman-priestess in her village threw the tiles and discovered that something bad was going to happen. A raiding party was coming. There was no point in fighting them. They would burn down everyone's houses and take the young men and women for slaves. And it was even worse than that. There was going to be an earthquake as well, which was bad news because usually, when raiders showed up, the village went down under the hill for a night and when they came out again the raiders would have been gone for months or decades or even a hundred years. But this earthquake was going to split the hill right open.

The people under the hill were in trouble. Their home would be destroyed, and they would be doomed to roam the face of the earth, weeping and lamenting their fate until the sun blew out and the sky cracked and the seas boiled and the people dried up and turned to dust and blew away. So the shaman-priestess went and divined some more, and the people under the hill told her to kill a black dog and skin it and use the skin to make a purse big enough to hold a chicken, an egg, and a cooking pot. So she did, and then the people under the hill made the inside of the purse big enough to hold all of the village and all of the people under the hill and mountains and forests and seas and rivers and lakes and orchards and a sky and stars and spirits and fabulous monsters and sirens and dragons and dryads and mermaids and beasties and all the little gods that the Baldeziwurlekistanians and the people under the hill worshipped.

"Your purse is made out of dog skin?" I said. "That's disgusting!"

"Little dear pet," Zofia said, looking wistful, "dog is delicious. To Baldeziwurlekistanians, dog is a delicacy."

Before the raiding party arrived, the village packed up all of their belongings and moved into the handbag. The clasp was made out of bone. If you opened it one way, then it was just a purse big enough to hold a chicken and an egg and a clay cooking pot, or else a pair of reading glasses and a library book and a pillbox. If you opened the clasp another way, then you found yourself in a little boat floating at the mouth of a river. On either side of you was forest, where the Baldeziwurlekistanian villagers and the people under the hill made their new settlement.

If you opened the handbag the wrong way, though, you found yourself in a dark land that smelled like blood. That's where the guardian of the purse (the dog whose skin had been sewn into a purse) lived. The guardian had no skin. Its howl made blood come out of your ears and nose. It tore apart anyone who turned the clasp in the opposite direction and opened the purse in the wrong way.

"Here is the wrong way to open the handbag," Zofia said. She twisted the clasp, showing me how she did it. She opened the mouth of the purse, but not very wide and held it up to me. "Go ahead, darling, and listen for a second."

I put my head near the handbag, but not too near. I didn't hear anything. "I don't hear anything," I said.

"The poor dog is probably asleep," Zofia said. "Even nightmares have to sleep now and then."

After he got expelled, everybody at school called Jake Houdini instead of Jake. Everybody except for me. I'll explain why, but you have to be patient. It's hard work telling everything in the right order.

Jake is smarter and also taller than most of our teachers. Not quite as tall as me. We've known each other since third grade. Jake has always been in love with me. He says he was in love with me even before third grade, even before we ever met. It took me a while to fall in love with Jake.

In third grade, Jake knew everything already, except how to make friends. He used to follow me around all day long. It made me so mad that I kicked him in the knee. When that didn't work, I threw his backpack out of the window of the school bus. That didn't work either, but the next year Jake took some tests and the school decided that he could skip fourth and fifth grade. Even I felt sorry for Jake then. Sixth grade didn't work out. When the sixth graders wouldn't stop flushing his head down the toilet, he went out and caught a skunk and set it loose in the boy's locker room.

The school was going to suspend him for the rest of the year, but instead Jake took two years off while his mother home-schooled him. He learned Latin and Hebrew and Greek, how to write sestinas, how to make sushi, how to play bridge, and even how to knit. He learned fencing and ballroom dancing. He worked in a soup kitchen and made a Super-8 movie about Civil War reenactors who play extreme croquet in full costume instead of firing off cannons. He started learning how to play guitar. He even wrote a novel. I've never read it—he says it was awful.

When he came back two years later, because his mother had cancer for the first time, the school put him back with our year, in seventh grade. He was still way too smart, but he was finally smart enough to figure out how to fit in. Plus he was good at soc-cer and he was really cute. Did I mention that he played guitar? Every girl in school had a crush on Jake, but he used to come home after school with me and play Scrabble with Zofia and ask her about Baldeziwurlekistan.

Jake's mom was named Cynthia. She collected ceramic frogs and knock-knock jokes. When we were in ninth grade, she had cancer again. When she died, Jake smashed all of her frogs. That was the first funeral I ever went to. A few months later, Jake's father asked Jake's fencing teacher out on a date. They got married right after the school expelled Jake for his AP project on Houdini. That was the first wedding I ever went to. Jake and I stole a bottle of wine and drank it, and I threw up in the swimming pool at the country club. Jake threw up all over my shoes.

So, anyway, the village and the people under the hill lived happily every after for a few weeks in the handbag, which they had tied around a rock in a dry well which the people under the hill had determined would survive the earthquake. But some of the Baldeziwurlekistanians wanted to come out again and see what was going on in the world. Zofia was one of them. It had been summer when they went into the bag, but when they came out again, and climbed out of the well, snow was falling and their village was ruins and crumbly old rubble. They walked through the snow, Zofia carrying the handbag, until they came to another village, one they'd never seen before. Everyone in that village was packing up their belongings and leaving, which gave Zofia and her friends a bad feeling. It seemed to be just the same as when they went *into* the handbag.

They followed the refugees, who seemed to know where they were going, and finally everyone came to a city. Zofia had never seen such a place. There were trains and electric lights and movie theaters, and there were people shooting each other. Bombs falling. A war was going on. Most of the villagers decided to climb right back inside the handbag, but Zofia volunteered to stay in the world and look after the handbag. She had fallen in love with movies and silk stockings and with a young man, a Russian deserter.

Zofia and the Russian deserter married and had many adventures and finally came to America, where my mother was born. Now and then Zofia would consult the tiles and talk to the people who lived in the handbag and they would tell her how best to avoid trouble and how she and her husband could make some money. Every now and then one of the Baldeziwurlekistanians, or one of the people from under the hill, came out of the handbag and wanted to go grocery shopping, or to a movie or an amusement park to ride on roller coasters, or to the library.

The more advice Zofia gave her husband, the more money they made. Her husband became curious about Zofia's handbag, because he could see that there was something odd about it, but Zofia told him to mind his own business. He began to spy on Zofia, and saw that strange men and women were coming in and out of the house. He became convinced that either Zofia was a spy for the Communists, or that she was having affairs. They fought and he drank more and more, and finally he threw away her divination tiles. "Russians make bad husbands," Zofia told me. Finally, one night while Zofia was sleeping, her husband opened the bone clasp and climbed inside the handbag.

"I thought he'd left me," Zofia said. "For almost twenty years I thought he'd left me and your mother and taken off for California. Not that I minded. I was tired of being married and cooking dinners and cleaning house for someone else. It's better to cook what I want to eat, and clean up when I decide to clean up. It was harder on your mother, not having a father. That was the part that I minded most.

"Then it turned out that he hadn't run away after all. He'd spent one night in the handbag and then come out again twenty years later, exactly as handsome as I remembered, and enough time had passed that I had forgiven him all the quarrels. We made up and it was all very romantic and then, when we had another fight the next morning, he went and kissed your mother, who had slept right through his visit, on the cheek, and climbed right back inside the handbag. I didn't see him again for another twenty years. The last time he showed up, we went to see *Star Wars* and he liked it so much that he went back inside the handbag to tell everyone else about it. In a couple of years they'll all show up and want to see it on DVD and all of the sequels too."

"Tell them not to bother with the prequels," I said.

The thing about Zofia and libraries is that she's always losing library books. She says that she hasn't lost them, and in fact that they aren't even overdue, really. It's just that even one week inside the faery handbag is a lot longer in library-world time. So what is she supposed to do about it? The librarians all hate Zofia. She's banned from using any of the branches in our area. When I was eight, she got me to go to the library for her and check out a bunch of biographies and science books and some Georgette Heyer novels. My mother was livid when she found out, but it was too late. Zofia had already misplaced most of them.

It's really hard to write about somebody as if they're really dead. I still think Zofia must be sitting in her living room, in her house, watching some old horror movie, dropping popcorn into her handbag. She's waiting for me to come over and play Scrabble.

Nobody is ever going to return those library books now.

My mother used to come home from work and roll her eyes. "Have you been telling them your fairy stories?" she'd say. "Genevieve, your grandmother is a horrible liar."

Zofia would fold up the Scrabble board and shrug at me and Jake. "I'm a wonderful liar," she'd say. "I'm the best liar in the world. Promise me you won't believe a single word."

But she wouldn't tell the story of the faery handbag to Jake. Only the old Baldeziwurlekistanian folktales and fairy tales about the people under the hill. She told him about how she and her husband made it all the way across Europe, hiding in haystacks and in barns, and how once, when her husband went off to find food, a farmer found her hiding in his chicken coop and tried to rape her, and how she managed to fight him off. (What she told me was she opened up the faery handbag in the way she'd showed me, and the dog came out and ate the farmer and all his chickens too.)

She was teaching Jake and me how to curse in Baldeziwurleki. I also know how to say I love you, but I'm not going to ever say it to anyone again, except to Jake, when I find him.

When I was eight, I believed everything Zofia told me. By the time I was thirteen, I didn't believe a single word. When I was fifteen, I saw a man come out of her house and get on Zofia's three-speed bicycle and ride down the street. His clothes looked funny. He was a lot younger than my mother and father, and even though I'd never seen him before, he was familiar. I followed him on my bike, all the way to the grocery store. I waited just past the checkout lanes while he bought peanut butter, Jack Daniel's, half a dozen instant cameras, and at least sixty packs of Reese's Peanut Butter Cups, three bags of Hershey's Kisses, a handful of Milky Way bars, and other stuff from the rack of checkout candy. While the checkout clerk was helping him bag up all of that chocolate, he looked up and saw me. "Genevieve?" he said. "That's your name, right?"

I turned and ran out of the store. He grabbed up the bags and ran after me. I don't even think he got his change back. I was still running away, and then one of the straps on my flip-flops popped out of the sole, the way they do, and that made me really angry so I just stopped. I turned around.

"Who are you?" I said.

But I already knew. He looked like he could have been my mom's younger brother. He was really cute. I could see why Zofia had fallen in love with him.

His name was Rustan. Zofia told my parents that he was an expert in Baldeziwurlekistanian folklore who would be staying with her for a few days. She brought him over for dinner. Jake was there too, and I could tell that Jake knew something was up. Everybody except my dad knew something was going on.

"You mean Baldeziwurlekistan is a real place?" my mother asked Rustan. "My mother is telling the truth?"

I could see that Rustan was having a hard time with that one. He obviously wanted to say that his wife was a horrible liar, but then where would he be? Then he couldn't be the person that he was supposed to be.

There were probably a lot of things that he wanted to say. What he said was, "This is really good pizza."

Rustan took a lot of pictures at dinner. The next day I went with him to get the pictures developed. He'd brought back some film with him, with pictures he'd taken inside the faery handbag, but those didn't come out well. Maybe the film was too old. We got doubles of the pictures from dinner so that I could have some too. There's a great picture of Jake, sitting outside on the porch. He's laughing, and he has his hand up to his mouth, like he's going to catch the laugh. I have that picture up on my computer, and also up on my wall over my bed.

I bought a Cadbury Creme Egg for Rustan. Then we shook hands and he kissed me once on each cheek. "Give one of those kisses to your mother," he said, and I thought about how the next time I saw him, I might be Zofia's age, and he would only be a few days older. The next time I saw him, Zofia would be dead. Jake and I might have kids. That was too weird.

I know Rustan tried to get Zofia to go with him, to live in the handbag, but she wouldn't.

"It makes me dizzy in there," she used to tell me. "And they don't have movie theaters. And I have to look after your mother and you. Maybe when you're old enough to look after the handbag, I'll poke my head inside, just long enough for a little visit."

I didn't fall in love with Jake because he was smart. I'm pretty smart myself. I know that smart doesn't mean nice, or even mean that you have a lot of common sense. Look at all the trouble smart people get themselves into.

I didn't fall in love with Jake because he could make maki rolls and had a black belt in fencing, or whatever it is that you get if you're good in fencing. I didn't fall in love with Jake because he plays guitar. He's a better soccer player than he is a guitar player.

Those were the reasons why I went out on a date with Jake. That, and because he asked me. He asked if I wanted to go see a movie, and I asked if I could bring my grandmother and Natalie and Natasha. He said sure and so all five of us sat and watched *Bring It On*, and every once in a while Zofia dropped a couple of Milk Duds or some popcorn into her purse. I don't know if she was feeding the dog, or if she'd opened the purse the right way, and was throwing food at her husband.

I fell in love with Jake because he told stupid knock-knock jokes to Natalie, and told Natasha that he liked her jeans. I fell in love with Jake when he took me and Zofia home. He walked her up to her front door and then he walked me up to mine. I fell in love with Jake when he didn't try to kiss me. The thing is, I was nervous about the whole kissing thing. Most guys think that they're better at it than they really are. Not that I think I'm a real genius at kissing, either, but I don't think kissing should be a competitive sport. It isn't tennis.

Natalie and Natasha and I used to practice kissing with each other. Not that we like each other that way, but just for practice. We got pretty good at it. We could see why kissing was supposed to be fun.

But Jake didn't try to kiss me. Instead he just gave me this really big hug. He put his face in my hair and he sighed. We stood there like that, and then finally I said, "What are you doing?"

"I just wanted to smell your hair," he said.

"Oh," I said. That made me feel weird, but in a good way. I put my nose up to his hair, which is brown and curly, and I smelled it. We stood there and smelled each other's hair, and I felt so good. I felt so happy.

Jake said into my hair, "Do you know that actor John Cusack?"

I said, "Yeah. One of Zofia's favorite movies is *Better Off Dead*. We watch it all the time."

"So he likes to go up to women and smell their armpits."

"Gross!" I said. "That's such a lie! What are you doing now? That tickles."

"I'm smelling your ear," Jake said.

Jake's hair smelled like iced tea with honey in it, after all the ice has melted.

Kissing Jake is like kissing Natalie or Natasha, except that it isn't just for fun. It feels like something there isn't a word for in Scrabble.

The deal with Houdini is that Jake got interested in him during Advanced Placement American History. He and I were both put in tenth grade history. We were doing biography projects. I was studying Joseph McCarthy. My grandmother had all sorts of stories about McCarthy. She hated him for what he did to Hollywood.

Jake didn't turn in his project—instead he told everyone in our AP class except for Mr. Streep (we call him Meryl) to meet him at the gym on Saturday. When we showed up, Jake reenacted one of Houdini's escapes with a laundry bag, handcuffs, a gym locker, bicycle chains, and the school's swimming pool. It took him three and a half minutes to get free, and this guy named Roger took a bunch of photos and then put the photos online. One of the photos ended up in the *Boston Globe*, and Jake got expelled. The really ironic thing was that while his mom was in the hospital, Jake had applied to MIT. He did it for his mom. He thought that way she'd have to stay alive. She was so excited about MIT. A couple of days after he'd been expelled, right after the wedding, while his dad and the fencing instructor were in Bermuda, he got an acceptance letter in the mail and that same afternoon, a phone call from this guy in the admissions office who explained why they had to withdraw the acceptance.

My mother wanted to know why I let Jake wrap himself up in bicycle chains and then watched while Peter and Michael pushed him into the deep end of the school pool. I said that Jake had a backup plan. Ten more seconds and we were all going to jump into the pool and open the locker and get him out of there. I was crying when I said that. Even before he got in the locker, I knew how stupid Jake was being. Afterward, he promised me that he'd never do anything like that again.

That was when I told him about Zofia's husband, Rustan, and about Zofia's handbag. How stupid am I?

So I guess you can figure out what happened next. The problem is that Jake believed me about the handbag. We spent a lot of time over at Zofia's, playing Scrabble. Zofia never let the faery handbag out of her sight. She even took it with her when she went to the bathroom. I think she even slept with it under her pillow.

I didn't tell her that I'd said anything to Jake. I wouldn't ever have told anybody else about it. Not Natasha. Not even Natalie, who is the most responsible person in all of the world. Now, of course, if the handbag turns up and Jake still hasn't come back, I'll have to tell Natalie. Somebody has to keep an eye on the stupid thing while I go find Jake.

What worries me is that maybe one of the Baldeziwurlekistanians or one of the people under the hill or maybe even Rustan popped out of the handbag to run an errand and got worried when Zofia wasn't there. Maybe they'll come looking for her and bring it back. Maybe they know I'm supposed to look after it now. Or maybe they took it and hid it somewhere. Maybe someone turned it in at the lost-and-found at the library and that stupid librarian called the FBI Maybe scientists at the Pentagon are examining the handbag right now. Testing it. If Jake comes out, they'll think he's a spy or a superweapon or an alien or something. They're not going to just let him go.

Everyone thinks Jake ran away, except for my mother, who is convinced that he was trying out another Houdini escape and is probably lying at the bottom of a lake somewhere. She hasn't said that to me, but I can see her thinking it. She keeps making cookies for me.

What happened is that Jake said, "Can I see that for just a second?"

He said it so casually that I think he caught Zofia off guard. She was reaching into the purse for her wallet. We were standing in the lobby of the movie theater on a Monday morning. Jake was behind the snack counter. He'd gotten a job there. He was wearing this stupid red paper hat and some kind of apron-bib thing. He was supposed to ask us if we wanted to supersize our drinks.

He reached over the counter and took Zofia's handbag right out of her hand. He closed it and then he opened it again. I think he opened it the right way. I don't think he ended up in the dark place. He said to me and Zofia, "I'll be right back." And then he wasn't there anymore. It was just me and Zofia and the handbag, lying there on the counter where he'd dropped it.

If I'd been fast enough, I think I could have followed him. But Zofia had been guardian of the faery handbag for a lot longer. She snatched the bag back and glared at me. "He's a very bad boy," she said. She was absolutely furious. "You're better off without him, Genevieve, I think."

"Give me the handbag," I said. "I have to go get him."

"It isn't a toy, Genevieve," she said. "It isn't a game. This isn't Scrabble. He comes back when he comes back. If he comes back."

"Give me the handbag," I said. "Or I'll take it from you."

She held the handbag up high over her head, so that I couldn't reach it. I hate people who are taller than me. "What are you going to do now?" Zofia said. "Are you going to knock me down? Are you going to steal the handbag? Are you going to go away and leave me here to explain to your parents where you've gone? Are you going to say good-bye to your friends? When you come out again, they will have gone to college. They'll have jobs and babies and houses and they won't even recognize you. Your mother will be an old woman and I will be dead."

"I don't care," I said. I sat down on the sticky red carpet in the lobby and started to cry. Someone wearing a little metal name tag came over and asked if we were okay. His name was Missy. Or maybe he was wearing someone else's tag.

"We're fine," Zofia said. "My granddaughter has the flu."

She took my hand and pulled me up. She put her arm around me and we walked out of the theater. We never even got to see the stupid movie. We never got to see another movie together. I don't ever want to go see another movie. The problem is, I don't want to see unhappy endings. And I don't know if I believe in the happy ones.

"I have a plan," Zofia said. "I will go find Jake. You will stay here and look after the handbag."

"You won't come back either," I said. I cried even harder. "Or if you do, I'll be like a hundred years old and Jake will still be sixteen."

"Everything will be okay," Zofia said. I wish I could tell you how beautiful she looked right then. It didn't matter if she was lying or if she actually knew that everything was going to be okay. The important thing was how she looked when she said it. She said, with absolute certainty, or maybe with all the skill of a very skillful liar, "My plan will work. First we go to the library, though. One of the people under the hill just brought back an Agatha Christie mystery, and I need to return it."

"We're going to the library?" I said. "Why don't we just go home and play Scrabble for a while." You probably think I was just being sarcastic here, and I *was* being sarcastic. But Zofia gave me a sharp look. She knew that if I was being sarcastic my brain was working again. She knew that I knew she was stalling for time. She knew that I was coming up with my own plan, which was a lot like Zofia's plan, except that I was the one who went into the handbag. *How* was the part I was working on.

"We could do that," she said. "Remember, when you don't know what to do, it never hurts to play Scrabble. It's like reading the I Ching or tea leaves."

"Can we please just hurry?" I said.

Zofia just looked at me. "Genevieve, we have plenty of time. If you're going to look after the handbag, you have to remember that. You have to be patient. Can you be patient?"

"I can try," I told her. I'm trying, Zofia. I'm trying really hard. But it isn't fair. Jake is off having adventures and talking to talking animals, and who knows, learning how to fly and some beautiful three-thousand-year-old girl from under the hill is teaching him how to speak fluent Baldeziwurleki. I bet she lives in a house that runs around on chicken legs, and she tells Jake that she'd love to hear him play something on the guitar. Maybe you'll kiss her, Jake, because she's put a spell on you. But whatever you do, don't go up into her house. Don't fall asleep in her bed. Come back soon, Jake, and bring the handbag with you.

I hate those movies, those books, where some guy gets to go off and have adventures and meanwhile the girl has to stay home and wait. I'm a feminist. I subscribe to *Bust* magazine, and I watch *Buffy* reruns. I don't believe in that kind of shit.

We hadn't been in the library for five minutes before Zofia picked up a biography of Carl Sagan and dropped it in her purse. She was definitely stalling for time. She was trying to come up with a plan that would counteract the plan that she knew I was planning. I wondered what she thought I was planning. It was probably much better than anything I could come up with.

"Don't do that!" I said.

"Don't worry," Zofia said. "Nobody was watching."

"I don't care if nobody saw! What if Jake's sitting there in the boat, or what if he was coming back and you just dropped it on his head!"

"It doesn't work that way," Zofia said. Then she said, "It would serve him right, anyway."

That was when the librarian came up to us. She had a nametag on as well. I was so sick of people and their stupid nametags. I'm not even going to tell you what her name was. "I saw that," the librarian said.

"Saw what?" Zofia said. She smiled down at the librarian, like she was Queen of the Library, and the librarian were a petitioner.

The librarian stared hard at her. "I know you," she said, almost sounding awed, like she was a weekend birdwatcher who had just seen Bigfoot. "We have your picture on the office wall. You're Ms. Swink. You aren't allowed to check out books here."

"That's ridiculous," Zofia said. She was at least two feet taller than the librarian. I felt a bit sorry for the librarian. After all, Zofia had just stolen a seven-day book. She probably wouldn't return it for a hundred years. My mother has always made it clear that it's my job to protect other people from Zofia. I guess I was Zofia's guardian before I became the guardian of the handbag.

The librarian reached up and grabbed Zofia's handbag. She was small but she was strong. She jerked the handbag and Zofia stumbled and fell back against a work desk. I couldn't believe it. Everyone except for me was getting a look at Zofia's handbag. What kind of guardian was I going to be?

The librarian said, "I saw you put a book in here. Right here." She opened the handbag and peered inside.

"Genevieve," Zofia said. She held my hand very tightly, and I looked at her. She looked wobbly and pale. She said, "I feel very bad about all of this. Tell your mother I said so."

Then she said one last thing, but I think it was in Baldeziwurleki.

Out of the handbag came a long, lonely, ferocious, utterly hopeless scream of rage. I don't ever want to hear that noise again. Everyone in the library looked up. The librarian made a choking noise and threw Zofia's handbag away from her. A little trickle of blood came out of her nose and a drop fell on the floor. What I thought at first was that it was just plain luck that the handbag was closed when it landed. Later on I was trying to figure out what Zofia said. My Baldeziwurleki isn't very good, but I think she was saying something like "Figures. Stupid librarian. I have to go take care of that damn dog." So maybe that's what happened. Maybe Zofia sent part of herself in there with the skinless dog. Maybe she fought it and won and closed the handbag. Maybe she made friends with it. I mean, she used to feed it popcorn at the movies. Maybe she's still in there.

What happened in the library was Zofia sighed a little and closed her eyes. I helped her sit down in a chair, but I don't think she was really there anymore. I rode with her in the ambulance, when the ambulance finally showed up, and I swear I didn't even think about the handbag until my mother showed up. I didn't say a word. I just left her there in the hospital with Zofia, who was on a respirator, and I ran all the way back to the library. But it was closed. So I ran all the way back again, to the hospital, but you already know what happened, right? Zofia died. I hate writing that. My tall, funny, beautiful, book-stealing, Scrabble-playing, story-telling grandmother died.

But you never met her. You're probably wondering about the handbag. What happened to it. I put up signs all over town, like Zofia's handbag was some kind of lost dog, but nobody ever called.

So that's the story so far. Not that I expect you to believe any of it. Last night Natalie and Natasha came over and we played Scrabble. They don't really like Scrabble, but they feel like it's their job to cheer me up. I won. After they went home, I flipped all the tiles upside down and then I started picking them up in groups of seven. I tried to ask a question, but it was hard to pick just one. The words I got weren't so great either, so I decided that they weren't English words. They were Baldeziwurleki words.

Once I decided that, everything became perfectly clear. First I put down "kirif" which means "happy news," and then I got a *b*, an *o*, an *l*, an *e*, an *f*, another *i*, an *s*, and a *z*. So then I could make "kirif" into "bolekirifisz," which could mean "the happy result of a combination of diligent effort and patience."

I would find the faery handbag. The tiles said so. I would work the clasp and go into the handbag and have my own adventures and would rescue Jake. Hardly any time would have gone by before we came back out of the handbag. Maybe I'd even make friends with that poor dog and get to say good-bye, for real, to Zofia. Rustan would show up again and be really sorry that he'd missed Zofia's funeral and this time he would be brave enough to tell my mother the whole story. He would tell her that he was her father. Not that she would believe him. Not that you should believe this story. Promise me that you won't believe a word.

First they played Go Fish, and then they played
Crazy Eights, and then they made the babysitter into
a mummy by putting shaving cream on her arms
and legs, and wrapping her in toilet paper.

THE SPECIALIST'S HAT

"WHEN YOU'RE DEAD," Samantha says, "you don't have to brush your teeth . . ."

"When you're Dead," Claire says, "you live in a box, and it's always dark, but you're not ever afraid."

Claire and Samantha are identical twins. Their combined age is twenty years, four months, and six days. Claire is better at being Dead than Samantha.

The babysitter yawns, covering up her mouth with a long white hand. "I said to brush your teeth and that it's time for bed," she says. She sits crosslegged on the flowered bedspread between them. She has been teaching them a card game called Pounce, which involves three decks of cards, one for each of them. Samantha's deck is missing the Jack of Spades and the Two of Hearts, and Claire keeps on cheating. The babysitter wins anyway. There are still flecks of dried shaving cream and toilet paper on her arms. It is hard to tell how old she is—at first they thought she must be a grownup, but now she hardly looks older than they. Samantha has forgotten the babysitter's name.

Claire's face is stubborn. "When you're Dead," she says, "you stay up all night long."

"When you're dead," the babysitter snaps, "it's always very cold and damp, and you have to be very, very quiet or else the Specialist will get you."

"This house is haunted," Claire says.

"I know it is," the babysitter says. "I used to live here."

Something is creeping up the stairs,
Something is standing outside the door,
Something is sobbing, sobbing in the dark;
Something is sighing across the floor.

Claire and Samantha are spending the summer with their father, in the house called Eight Chimneys. Their mother is dead. She has been dead for exactly 282 days.

Their father is writing a history of Eight Chimneys and of the poet Charles Cheatham Rash, who lived here at the turn of the century, and who ran away to sea when he was thirteen and returned when he was thirty-eight. He married, fathered a child, wrote three volumes of bad, obscure poetry and an even worse and more obscure novel, *The One Who Is Watching Me Through the Window*, before disappearing again in 1907, this time for good. Samantha and Claire's father says that some of the poetry is actually quite readable and at least the novel isn't very long.

When Samantha asked him why he was writing about Rash, he replied that no one else had and why didn't she and Samantha go play outside. When she pointed out that she was Samantha, he just scowled and said how could he be expected to tell them apart when they both wore blue jeans and flannel shirts, and why couldn't one of them dress all in green and the other in pink?

Claire and Samantha prefer to play inside. Eight Chimneys is as big as a castle, but dustier and darker than Samantha imagines a castle would be. There are more sofas, more china shepherdesses with chipped fingers, fewer suits of armor. No moat.

The house is open to the public, and, during the day, people—families—driving along the Blue Ridge Parkway will stop to tour the grounds and the first story; the third story belongs to Claire and Samantha. Sometimes they play explorers, and sometimes they follow the caretaker as he gives tours to visitors. After a few weeks, they have memorized his lecture, and they mouth it along with him. They help him sell postcards and copies of Rash's poetry to the tourist families who come into the little gift shop.

When the mothers smile at them and say how sweet they are, they stare back and don't say anything at all. The dim light in the house makes the mothers look pale and flickery and tired. They leave Eight Chimneys, mothers and families, looking not quite as real as they did before they paid their admissions, and of course Claire and Samantha will never see them again, so maybe they aren't real. Better to stay inside the house, they want to tell the families, and if you must leave, then go straight to your cars.

The caretaker says the woods aren't safe.

Their father stays in the library on the second story all morning, typing, and in the afternoon he takes long walks. He takes his pocket recorder along with him and a hip flask of Gentleman Jack, but not Samantha and Claire.

The caretaker of Eight Chimneys is Mr. Coeslak. His left leg is noticeably shorter than his right. He wears one stacked heel. Short black hairs grow out of his ears and his nostrils and there is no hair at all on top of his head, but he's given Samantha and Claire permission to explore the whole of the house. It was Mr. Coeslak who told them that there are copperheads in the woods, and that the house is haunted. He says they are all, ghosts and snakes, a pretty bad-tempered lot, and Samantha and Claire should stick to the marked trails, and stay out of the attic.

Mr. Coeslak can tell the twins apart, even if their father can't; Claire's eyes are grey, like a cat's fur, he says, but Samantha's are *gray*, like the ocean when it has been raining.

Samantha and Claire went walking in the woods on the second day that they were at Eight Chimneys. They saw something. Samantha thought it was a woman, but Claire said it was a snake. The staircase that goes up to the attic has been locked. They peeked through the keyhole, but it was too dark to see anything.

And so he had a wife, and they say she was real pretty. There was another man who wanted to go with her, and first she wouldn't, because she was afraid of her husband, and then she did. Her husband found out, and they say he killed a snake and got some of this snake's blood and put it in some whiskey and gave it to her. He had learned this from an island man who had been on a ship with him. And in about six months snakes created in her and they got between her meat and the skin. And they say you could just see them running up and down her legs. They say she was just hollow to the top of her body, and it kept on like that till she died. Now my daddy said he saw it.

—An Oral History of Eight Chimneys

Eight Chimneys is over two hundred years old. It is named for the eight chimneys that are each big enough that Samantha and Claire can both fit in one fireplace. The chimneys are red brick, and on each floor there are eight fireplaces, making a total of twenty-four. Samantha imagines the chimney stacks stretching like stout red tree trunks, all the way up through the slate roof of the house. Beside each fireplace is a black firedog and a set of wrought iron pokers shaped like snakes. Claire and Samantha pretend to duel with the snake-pokers before the fireplace in their bedroom on the third floor. Wind rises up the back of the chimney. When they stick their faces in, they can feel the air rushing damply upwards. The flue smells old and sooty and wet, like stones from a river.

Their bedroom was once the nursery. They sleep together in a poster bed that resembles a ship with four masts. It smells of mothballs, and Claire kicks in her sleep. Charles Cheatham Rash slept here when he was a little boy, and also his daughter. She disappeared when her father did. It might have been gambling debts. They may have moved to New Orleans. She was fourteen years old, Mr. Coeslak said. What was her name, Claire asked. What happened to her mother, Samantha wanted to know. Mr. Coeslak closed his eyes in an almost wink. Mrs. Rash had died the year before her husband and daughter disappeared, he said, of a mysterious wasting disease. He can't remember the name of the poor little girl, he said.

Eight Chimneys has exactly one hundred windows, all still with the original wavery panes of handblown glass. With so many windows, Samantha thinks, Eight Chimneys should always be full of light, but instead the trees press close against the house, so that the rooms on the first and second story—even the third-story rooms—are green and dim, as if Samantha and Claire are living deep under the sea. This is the light that makes the tourists into ghosts. In the morning, and again towards evening, a fog settles in around the house. Sometimes it is grey like Claire's eyes, and sometimes it is gray, like Samantha's eyes.

I met a woman in the wood,
Her lips were two red snakes.
She smiled at me, her eyes were lewd
And burning like a fire.

A few nights ago, the wind was sighing in the nursery chimney. Their father had already tucked them in and turned off the light. Claire dared Samantha to stick her head into the fireplace, in the dark, and so she did. The cold wet air licked at her face and it almost sounded like voices talking low, muttering. She couldn't quite make out what they were saying.

Their father has mostly ignored Claire and Samantha since they arrived at Eight Chimneys. He never mentions their mother. One evening they heard him shouting in the library, and when they came downstairs, there was a large sticky stain on the desk, where a glass of whiskey had been knocked over. It was looking at me, he said, through the window. It had orange eyes.

Samantha and Claire refrained from pointing out that the library is on the second story.

At night, their father's breath has been sweet from drinking, and he is spending more and more time in the woods, and less in the library. At dinner, usually hot dogs and baked beans from a can, which they eat off of paper plates in the first floor dining room, beneath the Austrian chandelier (which has exactly 632 leaded crystals shaped like teardrops) their father recites the poetry of Charles Cheatham Rash, which neither Samantha nor Claire cares for.

He has been reading the ship diaries that Rash kept, and he says he has discovered proof in them that Rash's most famous poem, "The Specialist's Hat," is not a poem at all, and in any case, Rash didn't write it. It is something one of the men on the whaler used to say, to conjure up a whale. Rash simply copied it down and stuck an end on it and said it was his.

The man was from Mulatuppu, which is a place neither Samantha nor Claire has ever heard of. Their father says that the man was supposed to be some sort of magician, but he drowned shortly before Rash came back to Eight Chimneys. Their father says that the other sailors wanted to throw the magician's chest overboard, but Rash persuaded them to let him keep it until he could be put ashore, with the chest, off the coast of North Carolina.

The specialist's hat makes a noise like an agouti;
The specialist's hat makes a noise like a collared peccary;
The specialist's hat makes a noise like a white-lipped peccary;
The specialist's hat makes a noise like a tapir;
The specialist's hat makes a noise like a rabbit;
The specialist's hat makes a noise like a squirrel;
The specialist's hat makes a noise like a curassow;
The specialist's hat moans like a whale in the water;
The specialist's hat moans like the wind in my wife's hair;
The specialist's hat makes a noise like a snake;
I have hung the hat of the specialist upon my wall.

The reason that Claire and Samantha have a babysitter is that their father met a woman in the woods. He is going to see her tonight, and they are going to have a picnic supper and look at the stars. This is the time of year when the Perseids can be seen, falling across the sky on clear nights. Their father said that he has been walking with the woman every afternoon. She is a distant relation of Rash and besides, he said, he needs a night off and some grownup conversation.

Mr. Coeslak won't stay in the house after dark, but he agreed to find someone to look after Samantha and Claire. Then their father couldn't find Mr. Coeslak, but the babysitter showed up precisely at seven o'clock. The babysitter, whose name neither twin quite caught, wears a blue cotton dress with short floaty sleeves. Both Samantha and Claire think she is pretty in an old-fashioned sort of way.

They were in the library with their father, looking up Mulatuppu in the red leather atlas, when she arrived. She didn't knock on the front door, she simply walked in and then up the stairs, as if she knew where to find them.

Their father kissed them good-bye, a hasty smack, told them to be good and he would take them into town on the weekend to see the Disney film. They went to the window to watch as he walked into the woods. Already it was getting dark and there were fireflies, tiny yellow-hot sparks in the air. When their father had entirely disappeared into the trees, they turned around and stared at the babysitter instead. She raised one eyebrow. "Well," she said. "What sort of games do you like to play?"

Widdershins around the chimneys,
Once, twice, again.
The spokes click like a clock on the bicycle;
They tick down the days of the life of a man.

First they played Go Fish, and then they played Crazy Eights, and then they made the babysitter into a mummy by putting shaving cream from their father's bathroom on her arms and legs, and wrapping her in toilet paper. She is the best babysitter they have ever had.

At nine-thirty, she tried to put them to bed. Neither Claire nor Samantha wanted to go to bed, so they began to play the Dead game. The Dead game is a let's pretend that they have been playing every day for 274 days now, but never in front of their father or any other adult. When they are Dead, they are allowed to do anything they want to. They can even fly by jumping off the nursery bed and just waving their arms. Someday this will work, if they practice hard enough.

The Dead game has three rules.

One. Numbers are significant. The twins keep a list of important numbers in a green address book that belonged to their mother. Mr. Coeslak's tour has been a good source of significant amounts and tallies: they are writing a tragical history of numbers.

Two. The twins don't play the Dead game in front of grown-ups. They have been summing up the babysitter, and have decided that she doesn't count. They tell her the rules.

Three is the best and most important rule. When you are Dead, you don't have to be afraid of anything. Samantha and Claire aren't sure who the Specialist is, but they aren't afraid of him.

To become Dead, they hold their breath while counting to 35, which is as high as their mother got, not counting a few days.

"You never lived here," Claire says. "Mr. Coeslak lives here."

"Not at night," says the babysitter. "This was my bedroom when I was little."

"Really?" Samantha says. Claire says, "Prove it."

The babysitter gives Samantha and Claire a look, as if she is measuring them: how old, how smart, how brave, how tall. Then she nods. The wind is in the flue, and in the dim nursery light they can see the milky strands of fog seeping out of the fireplace.

"Go stand in the chimney," she instructs them. "Stick your hand as far up as you can, and there is a little hole on the left side, with a key in it."

Samantha looks at Claire, who says, "Go ahead." Claire is fifteen minutes and some few uncounted seconds older than Samantha, and therefore gets to tell Samantha what to do. Samantha remembers the muttering voices and then reminds herself that she is Dead. She goes over to the fireplace and ducks inside.

When Samantha stands up in the chimney, she can only see the very edge of the room. She can see the fringe of the mothy blue rug, and one bed leg, and beside it, Claire's foot, swinging back and forth like a metronome. Claire's shoelace has come undone and there is a Band-Aid on her ankle. It all looks very pleasant and peaceful from inside the chimney, like a dream, and for a moment she almost wishes she didn't have to be Dead. But it's safer, really.

She sticks her left hand up as far as she can reach, trailing it along the crumbly wall, until she feels an indentation. She thinks about spiders and severed fingers, and rusty razorblades, and then she reaches inside. She keeps her eyes lowered, focused on the corner of the room and Claire's twitchy foot.

Inside the hole, there is a tiny cold key, its teeth facing outward. She pulls it out, and ducks back into the room. "She wasn't lying," she tells Claire.

"Of course I wasn't lying," the babysitter says. "When you're Dead, you're not allowed to tell lies."

"Unless you want to," Claire says.

Dreary and dreadful beats the sea at the shore.
Ghastly and dripping is the mist at the door.
The clock in the hall is chiming one, two, three, four.
The morning comes not, no, never, no more.

Samantha and Claire have gone to camp for three weeks every summer since they were seven. This year their father didn't ask them if they wanted to go back and, after discussing it, they decided that it was just as well. They didn't want to have to explain to all their friends how they were half-orphans now. They are used to being envied, because they are identical twins. They don't want to be pitiful.

It has not even been a year, but Samantha realizes that she is forgetting what her mother looked like. Not her mother's face so much as the way she smelled, which was something like dry hay and something like Chanel No. 5, and like something else too. She can't remember whether her mother had gray eyes, like her, or grey eyes, like Claire. She doesn't dream about her mother anymore, but she does dream about Prince Charming, a bay whom she once rode in the horse show at her camp. In the dream, Prince Charming did not smell like a horse at all. He smelled like Chanel No. 5. When she is Dead, she can have all the horses she wants, and they all smell like Chanel No. 5.

"Where does the key go to?" Samantha says.

The babysitter holds out her hand. "To the attic. You don't really need it, but taking the stairs is easier than the chimney. At least the first time."

"Aren't you going to make us go to bed?" Claire says.

The babysitter ignores Claire. "My father used to lock me in the attic when I was little, but I didn't mind. There was a bicycle up there and I used to ride it around and around the chimneys until my mother let me out again. Do you know how to ride a bicycle?"

"Of course," Claire says.

"If you ride fast enough, the Specialist can't catch you."

"What's the Specialist?" Samantha says. Bicycles are okay, but horses can go faster.

"The Specialist wears a hat," says the babysitter. "The hat makes noises."

She doesn't say anything else.

When you're dead, the grass is greener
Over your grave. The wind is keener.
Your eyes sink in, your flesh decays. You
Grow accustomed to slowness; expect delays.

The attic is somehow bigger and lonelier than Samantha and Claire thought it would be. The babysitter's key opens the locked door at the end of the hallway, revealing a narrow set of stairs. She waves them ahead and upwards.

It isn't as dark in the attic as they had imagined. The oaks that block the light and make the first three stories so dim and green and mysterious during the day don't reach all the way up. Extravagant moonlight, dusty and pale, streams in the angled dormer windows. It lights the length of the attic, which is wide enough to hold a softball game in, and lined with trunks where Samantha imagines people could sit, could be hiding and watching. The ceiling slopes down, impaled upon the eight thick-waisted chimney stacks. The chimneys seem too alive, somehow, to be contained in this empty, neglected place; they thrust almost angrily through the roof and attic floor. In the moonlight they look like they are breathing. "They're so beautiful," she says.

"Which chimney is the nursery chimney?" Claire says.

The babysitter points to the nearest right-hand stack. "That one," she says. "It runs up through the ballroom on the first floor, the library, the nursery."

Hanging from a nail on the nursery chimney is a long black object. It looks lumpy and heavy, as if it were full of things. The babysitter takes it down, twirls it on her finger. There are holes in the black thing and it whistles mournfully as she spins it. "The Specialist's hat," she says.

"That doesn't look like a hat," says Claire. "It doesn't look like anything at all." She goes to look through the boxes and trunks that are stacked against the far wall.

"It's a special hat," the babysitter says. "It's not supposed to look like anything. But it can sound like anything you can imagine. My father made it."

"Our father writes books," Samantha says.

"My father did too." The babysitter hangs the hat back on the nail. It curls blackly against the chimney. Samantha stares at it. It nickers at her. "He was a bad poet, but he was worse at magic."

Last summer, Samantha wished more than anything that she could have a horse. She thought she would have given up anything for one—even being a twin was not as good as having a horse. She still doesn't have a horse, but she doesn't have a mother either, and she can't help wondering if it's her fault. The hat nickers again, or maybe it is the wind in the chimney.

"What happened to him?" Claire asks.

"After he made the hat, the Specialist came and took him away. I hid in the nursery chimney while it was looking for him, and it didn't find me."

"Weren't you scared?"

There is a clattering, shivering, clicking noise. Claire has found the babysitter's bike and is dragging it towards them by the handlebars. The babysitter shrugs. "Rule number three," she says.

Claire snatches the hat off the nail. "I'm the Specialist!" she says, putting the hat on her head. It falls over her eyes, the floppy shapeless brim sewn with little asymmetrical buttons that flash and catch at the moonlight like teeth. Samantha looks again and sees that they are teeth. Without counting, she suddenly knows that there are exactly 52 teeth on the hat, and that they are the teeth of agoutis, of coatimundis, of white-lipped peccaries, and of the wife of Charles Cheatham Rash. The chimneys are moaning, and Claire's voice booms hollowly beneath the hat. "Run away, or I'll catch you. I'll eat you!"

Samantha and the babysitter run away, laughing as Claire mounts the rusty, noisy bicycle and pedals madly after them. She rings the bicycle bell as she rides, and the Specialist's hat bobs up and down on her head. It spits like a cat. The bell is shrill and thin, and the bike wails and shrieks. It leans first towards the right and then to the left. Claire's knobby knees stick out on either side like makeshift counterweights.

Claire weaves in and out between the chimneys, chasing Samantha and the babysitter. Samantha is slow, turning to look behind. As Claire approaches, she keeps one hand on the handlebars and stretches the other hand out towards Samantha. Just as she is about to grab Samantha, the babysitter turns back and plucks the hat off Claire's head.

"Shit!" the babysitter says, and drops it. There is a drop of blood forming on the fleshy part of the babysitter's hand, black in the moonlight, where the Specialist's hat has bitten her.

Claire dismounts, giggling. Samantha watches as the Specialist's hat rolls away. It picks up speed, veering across the attic floor, and disappears, thumping down the stairs. "Go get it," Claire says. "You can be the Specialist this time."

"No," the babysitter says, sucking at her palm. "It's time for bed."

When they go down the stairs, there is no sign of the Specialist's hat. They brush their teeth, climb into the ship-bed, and pull the covers up to their necks. The babysitter sits between their feet. "When you're Dead," Samantha says, "do you still get tired and have to go to sleep? Do you have dreams?"

"When you're Dead," the babysitter says, "everything's a lot easier. You don't have to do anything that you don't want to. You don't have to have a name, you don't have to remember. You don't even have to breathe."

She shows them exactly what she means.

When she has time to think about it (and now she has all the time in the world to think), Samantha realizes with a small pang that she is now stuck indefinitely between ten and eleven years old, stuck with Claire and the babysitter. She considers this. The number 10 is pleasing and round, like a beach ball, but all in all, it hasn't been an easy year. She wonders what 11 would have been like. Sharper, like needles maybe. She has chosen to be Dead, instead. She hopes that she's made the right decision. She wonders if her mother would have decided to be Dead, instead of dead, if she could have.

Last year they were learning fractions in school, when her mother died. Fractions remind Samantha of herds of wild horses, piebalds and pintos and palominos. There are so many of them, and they are, well, fractious and unruly. Just when you think you have one under control, it throws up its head and tosses you off. Claire's favorite number is 4, which she says is a tall, skinny boy. Samantha doesn't care for boys that much. She likes numbers. Take the number 8 for instance, which can be more than one thing at once. Looked at one way, 8 looks like a bent woman with curvy hair. But if you lay it down on its side, it looks like a snake curled with its tail in its mouth. This is sort of like the difference between being Dead, and being dead. Maybe when Samantha is tired of one, she will try the other.

On the lawn, under the oak trees, she hears someone calling her name. Samantha climbs out of bed and goes to the nursery window. She looks out through the wavy glass. It's Mr. Coeslak. "Samantha, Claire!" he calls up to her. "Are you all right? Is your father there?" Samantha can almost see the moonlight shining through him. "They're always locking me in the tool room. Goddamn spooky things," he says. "Are you there, Samantha? Claire? Girls?"

The babysitter comes and stands beside Samantha. The babysitter puts her finger to her lip. Claire's eyes glitter at them from the dark bed. Samantha doesn't say anything, but she waves at Mr. Coeslak. The babysitter waves too. Maybe he can see them waving, because after a little while he stops shouting and goes away. "Be careful," the babysitter says. "*He'll* be coming soon. It will be coming soon."

She takes Samantha's hand and leads her back to the bed, where Claire is waiting. They sit and wait. Time passes, but they don't get tired, they don't get any older.

Who's there?
Just air.

The front door opens on the first floor, and Samantha, Claire, and the babysitter can hear someone creeping, creeping up the stairs. "Be quiet," the babysitter says. "It's the Specialist."

Samantha and Claire are quiet. The nursery is dark and the wind crackles like a fire in the fireplace.

"Claire, Samantha, Samantha, Claire?" The Specialist's voice is blurry and wet. It sounds like their father's voice, but that's because the hat can imitate any noise, any voice. "Are you still awake?"

"Quick," the babysitter says. "It's time to go up to the attic and hide."

Claire and Samantha slip out from under the covers and dress quickly and silently. They follow her. Without speech, without breathing, she pulls them into the safety of the chimney. It is too dark to see, but they understand the babysitter perfectly when she mouths the word, *Up*. She goes first, so they can see where the finger-holds are, the bricks that jut out for their feet. Then Claire. Samantha watches her sister's foot ascend like smoke, the shoelace still untied.

"Claire? Samantha? Goddammit, you're scaring me. Where are you?" The Specialist is standing just outside the half-open door. "Samantha? I think I've been bitten by something. I think I've been bitten by a goddamn snake." Samantha hesitates for only a second. Then she is climbing up, up, up the nursery chimney.

ACKNOWLEDGMENTS

Thanks to my funny, forgiving, and unfailingly inspirational family—especially my cousin Bryan Jones who told me to write him into a story, my sister Holly Link who read many of these in early drafts, and my mother, Annabel Jones Link, who was my co-worker at B. Dolphin, a children's bookstore run by Mimi Levin and Janis Fields. Thanks to Elke and Penelope, who aren't old enough to read these yet. Thanks to the editors who originally published these stories: Ellen Datlow, Terri Windling, Jonathan Strahan, Eli Horowitz, Deborah Noyes, and, finally, my editor at Viking, Sharyn November, for her sharp eyes, her patience, her persistence. Inadequate thanks to Holly Black, Karen Joy Fowler, Molly Gloss, Leslie What, Betty Husted, Cassandra Clare, Gwenda Bond, Delia Sherman, Ellen Kushner, Sarah Smith, Jedediah Berry, Walter Jon Williams and the Rio Hondo Workshop, Richard Butner and John Kessel and the Sycamore Hill Workshop. Eternal thanks to my agent, Renee Zuckerbrot, and to Whitney Lee and Jenny Meyer. Thanks to Jim Hoover, for designing such a beautiful book. Thanks to Shaun Tan, whose illustrations have let me see some of these stories for the first time. Partial inspiration for "The Specialist's Hat" came from an exhibit at the Peabody Museum in Cambridge, MA: the longest poem in that story begins with a passage stuck up beside an empty exhibit case. Also adapted, for the same story, is a passage about snake whiskey from an outdoor folklore exhibit I visited in Raleigh, North Carolina. While working on this collection, I was supported by a grant from the National Endowment for the Arts. The stories in this collection owe a particular debt to the short stories and novels of Joan Aiken, Diana Wynne Jones, Robert Westall, Ursula K. Le Guin, and to the anthologies of Helen Hoke. Finally, thanks to my husband, Gavin, for the window display and everything since then.